PENGUIN TWENTIETH-CENTURY CLASSICS

ZAZIE IN THE METRO

An intellectual and polymath of the highest order, Raymond Queneau was, variously, a novelist, poet, essayist, lyricist, scriptwriter, translator, film director, and amateur mathematician. Born in Le Havre in 1903, he studied philosophy at the Sorbonne, was involved for a while with the Surrealist movement, joined the prestigious reading committee of the publishers Gallimard, and co-founded the Oulipo group, a literary workshop in existence to this day. His main achievement in the eyes of the public, though, was to write *Zazie in the Metro* (1959), the thirteenth of his fifteen novels. Adapted for film, stage, and comic-strip, it proved enormously popular—so much so that this leading light of the French literary establishment came to be overpoweringly associated in the public mind with his irreverent and entertaining creation. He died in 1976.

Zazie in the Metro was the second of the ten books by Raymond Queneau translated by Barbara Wright, the first being *Exercises in Style*. She has also translated fourteen books by Robert Pinget (including plays), several by Nathalie Sarraute and Michel Tournier (also including plays), and books by, among others, Pierre Albert-Briot, Elisabeth Badinter, Romain Gary, Jean Hamburger, Ludovic Janvier, Patrick Modiano, Pascal Quignard, Alain Robbe-Grillet, Jean Rouaud, and Tristan Tzara. She has also translated plays by Alfred Jarry, Arrabal, Beckett, Dubillard, Genet, Ionesco, Obaldia, Colin Serreau, Roland Topor, and others.

Gilbert Adair is the author of the novels *The Holy Innocents*, which won the Author's Club First Novel Award, *Love and Death on Long Island*, *The Death of the Author*, *The Key of the Tower*, and *A Closed Book*. He also wrote *Hollywood's Vietnam*, which analyzed the cinema's treatment of the Vietnam War; *Myths & Memories*, *The Postmodernist Always Rings Twice*, and *Surfing the Zeitgeist*, three collections of essays on British culture; *Flickers*, a celebration of the cinema's centenary; and two sequels to classics of children's literature, *Alice Through the Needle's Eye* and *Peter Pan and the Only Children*. He is the editor of *Movies* (Penguin, 1999). He lives in London and is frequently published as a journalist.

ZAZIE IN THE METRO

RAYMOND QUENEAU

TRANSLATED BY BARBARA WRIGHT
WITH AN INTRODUCTION BY GILBERT ADAIR

PENGUIN BOOKS

PENGUIN BOOKS
Published by the Penguin Group
Penguin Putnam Inc., 375 Hudson Street,
New York, New York 10014, U.S.A.
Penguin Books Ltd, 80 Strand, London WC2R 0RL, England
Penguin Books Australia Ltd, Ringwood, Victoria, Australia
Penguin Books Canada Ltd, 10 Alcorn Avenue,
Toronto, Ontario, Canada M4V 3B2
Penguin Books (N.Z.) Ltd, 182–190 Wairau Road,
Auckland 10, New Zealand

Penguin Books Ltd, Registered Offices:
Harmondsworth, Middlesex, England

First published in France as *Zazie dans le métro* by Librairie Gallimard 1959
This translation first published in Great Britain by The Bodley Head 1960
Published with an introduction in Penguin Classics (UK) 2000
Published in Penguin Books (USA) 2001

10 9 8 7 6 5 4 3 2 1

LIBRARY OF CONGRESS CATALOGING IN PUBLICATION DATA
Queneau, Raymond, 1903–1976.
[Zazie dans le métro. English]
Zazie in the metro / Raymond Queneau; translated by
Barbara Wright; with an introduction by Gilbert Adair.
p.   cm.
ISBN 0 14 21.8004 1 (pbk.: alk. paper)
I. Wright, Barbara, 1915–   II. Title.
PQ2633.U43 Z2513 2001
843'.912—dc21   2001045154

Printed in the United States of America
Set in Fournier

ὁ πλάσας ἠφάνισεν
Aristotle

Introduction

Zazie in the Metro, the thirteenth of Raymond Queneau's fifteen novels in all, was first published in France in 1959. Its success was immediate and unexpectedly considerable. Within just a month of publication fifty thousand copies had been purchased; and to date, without taking a dozen or so translations into account, sales of the novel have passed the million mark. It was filmed, by Louis Malle, in 1960, it has more than once been adapted to the stage (although never, surprisingly, as a Broadway musical comedy) and it was even reinvented as a comic-strip album. So powerfully, in fact, would Queneau come to be associated in the collective imagination with his most famous, or perhaps infamous, creation that, when he died in 1976, at the age of seventy-three, one Parisian newspaper headlined its obituary 'Zazie is in Mourning'.

Zazie, in short, became Queneau's Lolita. Although, like Nabokov (who had saddled himself with *his* nubile albatross only four years previously, in 1955), he was far from being a one-book author, and although a few long-standing champions of his work proved cliquishly minded to dismiss this particular effort not exactly as a potboiler but certainly as a slightly frivolous dissipation of his brilliance, as far as the wider general public is concerned Queneau was and has ever since remained Zazie, just as, for that same public, Nabokov is Lolita. *Zazie in the Metro*, which might after all be described, if somewhat reductively, as an intellectual *jeu d'esprit*, is thus also one of the last recorded examples of that terminally endangered species: an authentic popular classic.

But who, when he wasn't Zazie, was Raymond Queneau? Born in 1903 in Le Havre, he was a philosophy student at the Sorbonne during the first half of the twenties and a fellow-travelling Surrealist during the second half, until breaking with the group for reasons he would refer to as 'strictly personal'. In the thirties, he joined the ultra-prestigious reading committee of the publishers Gallimard and was one of several Parisian intellectuals (among the others were Georges Bataille and Jacques Lacan) to attend Alexandre Kojève's seminal lectures on Hegel at the Ecole des Hautes Etudes. (He would later edit Kojève's published notes.) The war over, he wrote witty lyrics for a number of popular songs, most memorably 'La Croqueuse de diamants' for the Roland Petit ballet of the same name. He scripted films for René Clément (*Monsieur Ripois*), Luis Buñuel (*La Mort en ce jardin*) and Alain Resnais (*Le Chant du styrène*, an amusing squib), and even directed a film of his own, *Le Lendemain*. He translated George du Maurier and Amos Tutuola. He co-founded, with François Le Lionnais, the celebrated Oulipo, short for 'Ouvroir de Littérature Potentielle', a literary workshop whose *raison d'être* was (*is*, rather: it continues to meet regularly) the invention of fiendish linguistic constraints. (Its most notable members, himself apart, were Georges Perec and Italo Calvino.) He wrote and published novels, volumes of poetry and collections of essays, as well as the quintessentially Oulipian *Exercices de style*, a droll, bestselling anthology of linguistic parodies. And he still found time to train himself as a decent amateur mathematician. He was, in other words, the type of multi-talented polymath possible only in France – or, more accurately, in Paris.

For his admirers and colleagues, then, Queneau was considerably more than merely 'Le Père de Zazie' (another obituary headline), and the exasperation of some of them at the way in which, in the case of *Zazie in the Metro*, the creation has tended to overshadow the creator should not be automatically ascribed to the intelligentsia's traditional fear, distrust and jealousy of popular success. Although Queneau's reputation has tended to suffer from his appearing to be something of a wag (France neither looks for nor expects humour from its great writers), he was nevertheless regarded by his peers as an intellectual – an ex-Surrealist *and* an ex-Marxist – of unimpeachable credentials. *Zazie* was to make him a star, like Brigitte Bardot or

Françoise Sagan, and it was that fact, along with the novel's incorrigible rompishness, that was so discombobulating.

It would not have happened in Britain, where there has existed such an exalted tradition of comic fiction – Fielding, Sterne, Austen, Dickens, the Grossmiths, Waugh, etc. – that no critic or academic, not even Leavis, has ever felt obliged to make embarrassed excuses for any writer belonging to it. But in the context of contemporary French literature Queneau was more or less unique. Not that that literature is devoid of humour – Proust, to mention only him, can be far funnier than any of the British writers cited above – but specifically comic novelists there have been next to none. And it's significant that even the maverick Queneau, possibly influenced by the prevailing intellectual solemnity, refused the epithet 'humourist' for himself, although it's one that arguably does apply to him up to a point. It's also significant that, when Roland Barthes published an essay in praise of him, he remarked that it was doubtless the fact that Queneau's fiction made its readers laugh out loud that had prevented it from being held in as high esteem as it deserved.

This is a point worth remembering by English readers who, for all the novel's wit and panache (as well as Barbara Wright's heroic translation), may wonder what the fuss is about or why it's so famous. Especially unhelpful are comparisons with Joyce. Unlike *Ulysses*, *Zazie* is not a *torrential* fiction. Its use of clichés, its mock-heroic parodies and, in particular, its phonetic-cum-demotic orthography is clearly meant to be neither exhaustive nor especially systematic: it can be, and quite patently has been, enjoyed by readers serenely untroubled by whether or not it extends the frontiers of literature. As an entertainment, which is what it was intended to be, it never sought to bury the conventional linear novel of the period – with its staid and proper elocution-class prose – merely cock a satirical snook at it, as we say. Queneau himself had too much at stake in the literary Establishment of his day to wish to take his linguistic experimentation further than he did; and probably, too, unlike Joyce, he did not have the temperament of a martyr. While writing *Zazie in the Metro*, he was, after all, reading new fiction for the Gallimard committee, keeping his (still mostly unpublished) diary up to date, presiding over the Oulipo's monthly sessions, attending private screenings of his friends' latest films and so forth. He was very much the man of letters, who, marvellous novelist that he was, never wrote a revolutionary work in his life.

What is *Zazie in the Metro* about? Not too much, really. Zazie Lalochère arrives in Paris with her mother from their vaguely dreary-sounding provincial village, is met at the Gare d'Austerlitz by her uncle, the ambiguous Gabriel, is consigned to his charge for thirty-six hours (spread over two nights and three days – it has all been timed), merrily scoots around the capital in the company of a variety of colourfully dubious characters, sweeping everyone and everything before her like one of those hurricanes to which women's names used sexistically to be given, but never succeeds in satisfying her heart's primary desire, which is to travel in the Metro. It has been closed because of a strike.

It's difficult to say why, but that brief synopsis – which is, really, the synopsis of a synopsis – makes it sound more like a film than a novel. And it's not merely the fact that it *was* filmed that makes it feel, in the reading, intrinsically cinematic – or the fact that the cutely malicious and definitely pre-pubescent Catherine Demongeot, who played Zazie in Malle's adaptation, is now, despite being significantly younger than the Zazie of the novel, everyone's Identikit image of the character. The year of the novel's publication, 1959, was equally the year of François Truffaut's *Les Quatre Cents Coups*, Jean-Luc Godard's *A bout de souffle* and Alain Resnais's *Hiroshima mon amour*, the year, in other words, in which the *nouvelle vague* erupted on the international cultural scene. A movie buff, Queneau would certainly have been conscious of this new aesthetic, and one's initial instinct is to presume that he came under its influence. Save for one startling fact: a book published in 1959 must have been written, at the very latest, in 1958 and probably even earlier than that. If, then, *Zazie in the Metro* can be regarded as what might be called 'a New Wave novel', what is extraordinary about it is that it's gestation actually predated the release of the films to which it bears so uncanny a resemblance.

Let's examine a few facets of that resemblance.

There is, in the first instance, *Zazie*'s narrative rhythm, the mercurial plotting and pacing, near-Voltairean in their unfussy speed and lightness, that whisk the characters from one end of Paris to another with little of the prosy, pragmatic connective tissue, the statutory passages of expositional description – what, in the cinema's terminology, are called establishing shots – that novelistic scene-shifting appears even now to require. This sort of ellipse can be compared to a filmic device that has come to be known, ever since it was pioneered by Godard in *A bout de souffle*, as the jump cut: a cut, brusque to the point of violence, between two shots that deliberately edits out the central section of some continuous action. As the reader will discover, Queneau often employs literary 'jump cuts' in *Zazie* – and, I repeat, at least a year before Godard was credited with inventing them for the cinema.

Then there is the manner in which Paris itself is evoked, metonymically, almost invariably in close-up, with the wider urban picture left in abeyance, 'off-screen'. Each of the novel's different locations, the boulevard Sebastopol, the rue Rambuteau, the place Pigalle, etc. (some of which are visited by the characters, others merely mentioned in the text), is defined, as would subsequently be true of the cinema of the *nouvelle vague*, by a single faintly cartoonish signifier, be it a corner café, a monument or a market stall. (Whimsically, one might propose that the Paris of *Zazie* is the ideogrammatic Paris of a child's board game, a variation on Ludo or Monopoly in which the player's goal is to reach the final square, the Metro.)

And the very fact that so much of the novel's action takes place 'on location', so to speak, links it with the New Wave films, one of whose defining characteristics was their directors' wish to get the camera, like some pasty-complexioned, nose-in-a-book youth, out of the house (or the studio) and into the open air. Although I have no statistical evidence at hand to support such a theory, I would be prepared to speculate that, in the vast majority of serious, ambitious French novels written in the late fifties (I exclude thrillers), almost all of the action takes place indoors – just as, in the majority of serious, 'ambitious' films against which the New Wave mutinied, the action tended to be confined to stagy and claustrophobic studio sets.

In as much the literal as the figurative sense, *Zazie* brought a gust of fresh air into French literature.

As for the dialogue's slangy neologisms, so unusual and provocative in a novel by a writer as reputable as Queneau (even if *Zazie* was by no means the first of his works to deploy them), they were very much the thing in the populist cinema of the period and, significantly, would later be parodied, usually with affection, by Godard, Truffaut and Chabrol in their paraphrases, sometimes larky and sometimes lugubrious, of the classic French gangster movie.

Which brings us to a more trivial yet telling filmic echo, the novel's last two-word sentence, spoken by Zazie herself (it would be unjust to divulge it here), which closes off the narrative like a curtain line or, more precisely, like the kind of verbal pirouette with which so many films over the years have been brought to a satisfyingly abrupt conclusion. To take only the most obvious example, it invites comparison with the celebrated 'Nobody's perfect!', probably the most beloved last line in cinema history, of Billy Wilder's *Some Like It Hot*, a film released, coincidentally, in that same eventful year of 1959.

Lastly (in an inventory that makes no claim to comprehensiveness), there is the curious fact that not one of the novel's characters has been accorded by his or her creator what one might call an interiority. These characters live on the page, and live vividly, by sole virtue of the external tics (and sometimes by a single tic) assigned to them by Queneau as though for all eternity, just as there exist in the film business prolific character actors who have contrived to spin out their entire careers on the systematic exploitation of just one eccentric trait.

One thinks of gentle Marceline, Gabriel's gentle companion, who remains gentle in everything she says and does, even in situations which scarcely lend themselves to self-effacing docility. (The actress who played her in the film version wore a quasi-permanent blush, a minor instance of how Malle had to rethink the novel in visual terms.) One thinks of the cobbler Gridoux, that gruff sage and autodidact ('ne sutor ultra crepidam'), who, even as the world goes mad around him, insists on keeping, as befits his profession (or, as he would see it, vocation), his two feet firmly on the ground. One thinks, above all, of Laverdure, Marceline's pet parrot, with its ritual, eternally reiterated and, of course, ultimately self-applicable catchphrase 'Talk, talk, that's all you can do', a running verbal gag of a type that again is much likelier to be found in films than in novels.

Zazie herself, however, unquestionably the main reason for the novel's unprecedented success with the general public, is the most striking example of this strange absence of characterial psychology. Not only has she been granted no interiority, she is not even blessed with much of an exteriority. We never, for example, discover her age, the colour of her hair or eyes, how she is dressed (until she finesses herself a pair of jeans), whether grown-ups consider her pretty or unprepossessing, or, indeed, anything of her outward physical appearance. Barthes went so far as to deny that she was a child at all, preferring to regard her infancy as a strictly linguistic construct, 'a form of abstraction which enables her to judge all language without ever having to mask her own psyche'. Maybe so. Yet, if thousands of readers warmed to her, it may equally be because they recognized in her – in her voice, I should say, since that was all they were given to work with – one of the most childlike of all human attributes: total self-interest.

Zazie *is* a child, triumphantly a child, because she is a bundle of desires (as one might refer to some overwrought acquaintance as 'a bundle of nerves'), and it is surely no coincidence that those desires of hers, poignantly dated as they may seem to us now, could almost be held up as emblems of the consumerist frenzy that was already, by the late fifties, in the process of transforming French society, the very same emblems to which the filmmakers of the *nouvelle vague* would be in thrall throughout the next decade: Coca-Cola, blue jeans and, naturally, the Metro.

Gilbert Adair

Zazie

Howcanaystinksotho, wondered Gabriel, exasperated. Ts incredible, they never clean themselves. It says in the paper that not eleven percent of the flats in Paris have bathrooms, doesn't surprise me, but you can wash without. They can't make much of an effort, all this lot around me. On the other hand, it's not as if they've been specially hand-picked from the dosses of Paris. Zno reason. They're only here by accident. You really can't assume that people who meet people at the Gare d'Austerlitz smell worse than people who meet people at the Gare de Lyon. No really, zno reason. All the same, what a smell.

Gabriel extirpated from his sleeve a mauve silk handkerchief and dabbed his boko with it.

'What on earth's that stench?' said a good lady out loud.

She wasn't thinking about herself when she said that, she wasn't so self-centred, she was referring to the perfume that emanated from the meussieu.

'That, dearie,' replied Gabriel, who was never at a loss when it came to repartee, 'is Barbouze, a perfume from the House of Fior.'

'Toughn't to be allowed, stinking people out like that,' continued the old bag, sure of her ground.

'If I understand you aright, dearie, you imagine that your natural perfume is sweeter than the roses. Well, you're wrong, dearie, you're wrong.'

'Hear that?' said the good lady to a little chap by her side, probably the one legally entitled to mount her. 'D'you hear how rude he's being to me, the dirty great pig?'

The little chap examined Gabriel's dimensions and said to himself he's a Tarzan, but Tarzans are always good-natured, never take advantage of their strength, that'd be a coward's trick. Cock o' the walk, he screeched:

'You stink, you gorilla.'

Gabriel sighed. Incitement to violence again. This coercion made him sick. Since the first hominization it had never stopped. However, what had to be had to be. Wasn't his fault if it was always the weaklings who gave everybody the balls-ache. Still, he'd give the gnat a chance.

'Say again,' says Gabriel.

A bit surprised that the stalwart should answer back, the little chap took his time, and concocted the following reply:

'Say what again?'

Not displeased with his turn of phrase, the little chap wasn't. Only the great hulk didn't let up, it leant over him and uttered this monophasic pentasyllable:

'Wottusaidjusnow.'

The little chap began to get apprehensive. Now was his time, now was the moment to forge some sort of verbal buckler. The first that came into his head was an alexandrine:

'And anyway who said that you could call me *tu*?'

'Yellow-belly,' retorted Gabriel with simplicity.

And he raised his arm as if he wanted to sock the little fellow one. Without labouring the point, the latter fell to the ground under his own steam, in the middle of all the people's legs. He felt a great urge to cry. Luckily, here comes the train into the station, which changes the landscape. The perfumed crowd casts its multiple eyes in the direction of the arrivals who are starting to parade past it, business men quick-marching at their head, with their brief-cases at the end of their arms as their only encumbrance and their air of knowing how to travel better than anyone else.

Gabriel looks into the distance; they're bound to be bringing up the rear, women always do bring up the rear; no, though, a little chick materializes and addresses him:

'I'm Zazie, I bet you're myyuncle Gabriel.'

'I am indeed,' says Gabriel, ennobling his tone. 'Yes, I'm your uncle.'

The kid cackles. Gabriel, smiling politely, takes her in his arms, he transports her to the level of his lips, he kisses her, she kisses him, he puts her down again.

'You smell gorgeous,' says the child.

'Fior's Barbouze,' explains the colossus.

'Will you put a bit behind my ears?'

'It's a man's perfume.'

'That's the little object,' says Jeanne Lalochère, turning up at last. 'You said you'd look after it, well, here it is.'

'That'll be all right,' says Gabriel.

'Can I really rely on you? I don't want her to get herself raped by the whole family, you know.'

'But mummuh, you know perfectly well that you came in just in time last time.'

'In any case,' says Jeanne Lalochère, 'I don't want it to happen again.'

'You don't need to worry,' says Gabriel.

'Good. Then I'll see you here the day after tomorrow in time for the six-sixty train.'

'On the departures side,' says Gabriel.

'Natürlich,' says Jeanne Lalochère, who had been occupied. 'By the way, how's your wife, all right?'

'Yes thank you. Won't you be coming to see us?'

'Shan't have time.'

'That's how she is when she's got a boy friend,' says Zazie, 'the family doesn't count any more.'

'Bye, love. Bye, Gaby.'

She beats it.

Zazie comments on the events:

'She's got it badly.'

Gabriel shrugs his shoulders. He says nothing. He seizes Zazie's suitcase.

Now he does say something.

'Let's go,' he says.

And he charges, scattering around him everything that happens to be in his trajectory. Zazie gallops behind.

5

'Unkoo,' she yells, 'are we going by metro?'

'No.'

'What d'you mean, no?'

She has come to a full stop. Gabriel likewise halts, turns round, puts the suitcase down and starts to iksplain:

'Well yes: no. Today, can't be done. Za strike.'

'Za strike?'

'Well yes: za strike. The metro, that eminently parisian means of transport, has fallen asleep under the ground, for the employees with their perforating punches have ceased to work.'

'Oo the bastards,' cries Zazie, 'oo the swine. To do that to me.'

'Snot only you they're doing it to,' says Gabriel, perfectly objective.

'Don't give a damn. Doesn't alter the fact that it's happening to me, me that was so happy, so pleased and everything to be going to be conveyed by metro. Blast, bloody hell.'

'Have to make the best of it, have to be reasonable,' said Gabriel whose remarks were sometimes tinged with a slightly Kantian Thomism.

And, passing on to the level of cosubjectivity, he added:

'And anyway we must get a move on. My time and patience may be inexhaustible, but Charley's aren't.'

'Oh! I know that one,' exclaimed Zazie, furious, 'I read it in the Almanach Vermot*.'

'Oh no,' said Gabriel, 'oh no, Charles is a pal and he has a cab and he's waiting for us, I booked it uswise, his cab, precisely on account of the strike. Got it? Tsgo.'

He reseized the suitcase with one hand and dragged Zazie along with the other.

Charles was in fact waiting for them, reading the bleeding hearts column of a weekly mag. He was looking for, and it was already quite some years that he had been looking for, a nice plump chicken to whom he could make a gift of the forty-five cherries of his

---

* (To be found in most French bourgeois households: a fanciful amalgam of *Old Moore's Almanack*, *Film Fun* and *The Girl Guide's Diary*, each page garnished with feeble jokes. – Translator's note.)

summers. But those such who, just like that, exposed their sufferings in this news-sheet, he always found them either too daft or too hideous. Perfidious or artful. He could smell out the mote in the beams of their lamentations and detect the potential cow in the most devastated doll.

'Hallo, ducks,' he said to Zazie without looking at her, carefully tidying his publication away beneath his buttocks.

'It's lousy, his old jalopy,' said Zazie.

'Get in,' said Gabriel, 'and don't be such a snob.'

'Snob my arse,' said Zazie.

'Funny little creature, your niece,' says Charles, and he pushes the syringe and causes the engine to revolve.

With a light but powerful hand, Gabriel shoves Zazie on to the back seat of the taks, then he installs himself by her side.

Zazie protests.

'You're squashing me,' she yells, mad with fury.

'Promising,' remarks Charles succinctly in a calm voice.

He starts up.

They drive for a bit, then Gabriel indicates the landscape with a magnificent gesture.

'Ah! Paris,' he utters, in an encouraging tone, 'what a beautiful city. Just look, eh, how beautiful it is.'

'Don't give a damn,' says Zazie, 'what *I* wanted was to go in the metro.'

'The metro!' bawls Gabriel, 'the metro!! well there it is!!!'

And he points to something in the air.

Zazie frowns. Shezon her guard.

'The metro?' she repeats. 'The metro,' she adds scornfully, 'it's underground, the metro. Well Ida know.'

'That one,' says Gabriel, 'is the elevated.'

'Well then, it's not the metro.'

'I'll ksplain,' says Gabriel. 'Sometimes it comes out of the ground and then later it rere-enters it.'

'Tripe.'

Gabriel feels helpless (gesture), then, wishing to change the subject, he points out something else they happen to be passing.

'How about that!' he roars, 'look!! the Panthéon!!!'

'The things you hear,' says Charles without turning round.

He was driving slowly so that the child could see the sights and improve her mind into the bargain.

'Maybe it isn't the Panthéon?' asks Gabriel.

There's something crafty about his question.

'No,' says Charles forcefully. 'No, no and no, it isn't the Panthéon.'

'Well what would it be then in your opinion?'

The craftiness of his tone becomes almost insulting to his interlocutor who, moreover, hastens to admit defeat.

'I don't really know,' says Charles.

'There. You see.'

'But it isn't the Panthéon.'

The thing is that Charles is pig-headed, as well.

'We'll ask a passer-by,' suggests Gabriel.

'Passers-by!' retorts Charles, 'they're all bleeding clots.'

'That's true enough,' says Zazie serenely.

Gabriel doesn't insist. He discovers a new subject to enthuse about.

'And that,' he exclaims, 'that's . . .'

But he's cut short by a eurequation from his brother-in-law.

'I've got it,' roars the latter. 'The thing we've just seen, twasn't the Panthéon, course it wasn't, it was the Gare de Lyon.'

'Maybe,' says Gabriel casually, 'but it's past history now, let's not talk about it any more, whereas that, Zazie, just have a look at that and see if it isn't a lovely lump of architecture, it's the Invalides . . .'

'You're talking through the back of your head,' says Charles, 'that's got nothing to do with the Invalides.'

'Well,' says Gabriel, 'if it isn't the Invalides, tell us whatitiz.'

'I don't know exactly,' says Charles, 'but at the very most it's the Reuilly Barracks.'

'You two,' says Zazie indulgently, 'you're funny little creatures.'

'Zazie,' declares Gabriel, assuming a majestic air which he effortlessly selects from his repertoire, 'if you'd really like to see the Invalides and the genuine tomb of the real Napoleon, I'll take you there.'

'Napoleon my arse,' retorts Zazie. 'I'm not in the least interested in that old windbag with his silly bugger's hat.'

'What *are* you interested in then?'

Zazie doesn't answer.

'Yes,' says Charles, with unexpected gentleness, 'what *are* you interested in?'

'The metro.'

Gabriel says: ah. Charles doesn't say anything. Then Gabriel goes back to what he was saying, and again says: ah.

'And when's this strike going to be over?' asks Zazie, her words bulging with ferocity.

'How should I know,' says Gabriel, 'I don't go in for politics.'

'Snot politics,' says Charles, 'it's a question of their daily bread.'

'What about you, msieu,' Zazie asks him, 'do you ever go on strike?'

'Huh, well, have to, to get the fares put up.'

'They ought to put them down, if anything, with an old crate like yours, they don't come any lousier. You didn't find it on the banks of the Marne by any chance?'

'We'll be there in a minute,' says Gabriel the peacemaker. 'There's the corner caff.'

'Which corner?' asks Charles ironically.

'The corner of my road where I live,' replies Gabriel ingenuously.

'Well then,' says Charles, 'tisn't that one.'

'Whaaat,' says Gabriel, 'you really mean to say it's not that one?'

'Oh no,' cries Zazie, 'you're not going to start all over again.'

'No, it isn't that one,' Charles answers Gabriel.

'You're quite right though,' says Gabriel as they pass the caff, 'that one I've never been in.'

'As a matter of interest, Unkoo,' says Zazie, 'when you talk crap like that, do you do it on purpose or can't you help it?'

'It's to make you laugh, my child,' replies Gabriel.

'Don't worry,' says Charles to Zazie, 'he doesn't do it on purrpuss.'

'It's not very funny,' says Zazie.

'The truth is,' says Charles, 'that sometimes he does it on purrpuss and sometimes he doesn't.'

'The truth!' exclaims Gabriel (gesture), 'as if you knew whatitiz. As if anyone in the world knew whatitiz. All that (gesture), all that's bogus: the Panthéon, the Invalides, the Reuilly Barracks, the corner caff, the whole lot. Yes, bogus.'

He adds, overwhelmed:

'Oh dear me, what a life!'

'D'you like to stop for a drink?' asks Charles.

'That's an idea.'

'At La Cave?'

'In Saint-Germain-des-Prés?' asks Zazie who's already quivering.

'Oh go on, young lady,' says Gabriel, 'what are you thinking of? It's completely out of date.'

'If you're trying to make out that I don't know what's what,' says Zazie, 'I might inform you that you're just a bloody old clotface.'

'You hear that?' says Gabriel.

'Well there you are,' says Charles, 'that's the younger generation for you.'

'The younger generation,' says Zazie, 'doesn't give a . . .'

'All right all right,' says Gabriel, 'we've got it. Shall we go to the caff on the corner?'

'On the proper corner,' says Charles.

'Yes,' says Gabriel. 'And after you'll stay and have dinner with us.'

'Wasn't that already fixed?'

'Yes.'

'Well then?'

'Well then, I'm confirming it.'

'There's no need to confirm it, since it was already fixed.'

'Well, let's say that I'm reminding you just in case you'd forgotten.'

'I hadn't forgotten.'

'Then you'll stay and have dinner with us.'

'Oh look here, hell,' says Zazie, 'are we ever going to have that drink?'

Gabriel extracts himself neatly and lithely from the taks. They all meet again round a table on the pavement. The waitress comes up without enthusiasm. Zazie immediately makes her wishes known:

'A cacocalo,' she requests.

'Haven't got any,' she gets answered.

'Well really,' exclaims Zazie, 'that's the end.'

She is indignant.

'I'll have a beaujolais,' says Charles.

'And I'll have a milk and grenadine,' says Gabriel. 'How about you?' he asks Zazie.

'Valready told her: a cacocalo.'

'She said they haven't got any.'

'Itza cacocalo I want.'

'You can want as much as you like,' says Gabriel with ikstreme patience, 'but you can see perfectly well that they haven't got any.'

'Why haven't you got any?' demands Zazie of the waitress.

'Well (gesture).'

'A shandy, Zazie,' suggests Gabriel, 'wouldn't you like that?'

'Itza cacocalo I want and nothing else.'

Everyone becomes thoughtful. The waitress scratches a thigh.

'Vgot some next door,' she finally says. 'At the Italian's.'

'Here,' says Charles, 'is my beaujolais coming?'

She goes to get it. Gabriel gets up, without comment. He disappears with celerity and is soon back with a bottle from whose neck two straws project. He puts this in front of Zazie.

'Here you are, love,' he says in a generous voice.

Without a word Zazie picks up the bottle and starts to play the bagpipes.

'There, you see,' says Gabriel to his pal, 'it wasn't difficult. With children, all you need is to understand 'em.'

2

'Here we are,' says Gabriel.

Zazie scrutinizes the house. She doesn't communicate her impressions.

'Well?' asked Gabriel. 'Will it do?'

Zazie made a sign which seemed to indicate that she was reserving her judgment.

'I,' said Charles, ''m going to see Turandot. I've got something to say to him.'

'I understand,' said Gabriel.

'What is there to understand?' asked Zazie.

Charles went down the five steps leading from the pavement to the La Cave café-restaurant, pushed open the door and made his way to the zinc counter which had been a wooden counter since the occupation.

'Hallo, Meussieu Charles,' said Mado Ptits-pieds, who was serving a customer.

'Hallo, Mado,' replied Charles without looking at her.

'That her?' asked Turandot.

'Crect,' replied Charles.

'She's bigger than I expected.'

'So what?'

'I don't like it. I told Gaby, I don't want any trouble in my place.'

'Here, give me a beaujolais.'

Turandot served him in meditative silence. Charles knocked back his beaujolais, wiped his moustache with the back of his hand, and then looked absent-mindedly in the direction of the outside world. To do this you had to raise your head, and then you only saw feet, ankles, trouser turn-ups, and sometimes, if you were very lucky, a whole dog, a dachshund. A cage hanging near the fanlight harboured a sad parrot. Turandot refilled Charles' glass and poured himself a nip. Mado Ptits-pieds came and installed herself behind the counter beside the boss and broke the silence.

'Meussieu Charles,' says she, 'yourra melancholic.'

'Melancholic my arse,' retorts Charles.

'Well I must say,' exclaimed Mado Ptits-pieds, 'you aren't very polite today.'

'It makes me laugh,' said Charles with a sinister air. 'That's how she talks, that little chit.'

'Don't understand,' said Turandot, not at all at his ease.

'It's perfectly simple,' said Charles. 'She can't say a word, that kid, without sticking my arse on to it.'

'And does she suit the action to the words?' asked Turandot.

'Not yet,' replied Charles gravely, 'but she soon will.'

'Oh no,' groaned Turandot, 'no, not that.'

He took hold of his head in both hands and made a futile show of trying to tear it off. Then he continued his speech in these terms:

'Bloody stinking hell, I don't want a little slut that talks such obsceneries in my place. I can see it coming, she'll corrupt the whole neighbourhood. A week from now . . .'

'She's only here for two or three days,' said Charles.

'It's too long!' cried Turandot. 'In two or three days she'll have had time to put her hand in the flies of all the old dodderers who honour me with their custom. I don't want any trouble, d'you hear, I don't want any trouble.'

The parrot, who was nibbling at one of his claws, lowered his gaze and, interrupting his toilet, chipped in.

'Talk,' said Laverdure, 'talk, that's all you can do.'

'He's quite right,' said Charles. 'After all *I*'m not the person to tell your troubles to.'

'He can go and bugger himself,' says Gabriel affectionately, 'but I can't help wondering why you had to tell him about the child's language.'

'I'm just frank,' says Charles. 'And anyway you can't disguise the fact that your niece is bloody badly brought up. Tell me, did *you* talk like that when you were a kid?'

'No,' replies Gabriel, 'but then I wasn't a little girl.'

'Dinner's ready,' says Marceline gently, bringing in the soup. 'Zazie' she calls gently, 'dinner's ready.'

She starts gently pouring the contents of the ladle into the plates.

'Aha,' says Gabriel with satisfaction, 'consommé.'

'Don't let's egzaggerate,' says Marceline gently.

Zazie finally comes and joins them. She sits down, with a blank look, noticing resentfully that she's hungry.

After the soup there was black pudding with pommes savoyardes, and then afterwards some foie gras (which Gabriel brought home from the cabaret, he just couldn't stop himself, when there was foie gras lying about right and theft), and then a very sweet sweet, and then some coffee distributed in cups, coffee on account of both Charles' and Gabriel's slavery was at night. Charles left immediately after the expected surprise of grenadine au kirsch, but Gabriel's work only started around eleven. He stretched his legs out under the table and even beyond, and smiled at Zazie who was sitting stiffly on her chair.

'Well, young lady,' he said casually, 'it's bed for us.'

'Who's "us"?' she asked.

'Well, you of course,' replied Gabriel falling into the trap. 'What time d'you go to bed at home?'

'Here and there's two different matters, I hope.'

'Yes,' said Gabriel, being understanding.

'That's why I got left here, so's it shouldn't be like there. Don't you think?'

'Yes.'

'Do you say yes just like that or do you really think so?'

Gabriel turned to Marceline, who was smiling.

'You see how well they reason, even at that age. Makes you wonder why people bother to send them to school.'

'Personally,' declared Zazie, 'I want to go to school until I'm sixty-five.'

'Until you're sixty-five?' repeated Gabriel, just a teensy bit surprised.

'Yes,' said Zazie, 'I want to be a teacher.'

'That's not a bad trade,' said Marceline gently. 'There's the pension.'

She put that in automatically because she always knew the right thing to say.

'Pension my arse,' said Zazie. 'Tisn't for the pension that I want to be a teacher.'

'No of course not,' said Gabriel, 'we thought as much.'

'Why is it then?' asked Zazie.

'You aksplain it to us.'

'Because you'd never guess, would you?'

'Well I must say, they know a thing or two, the youth of today,' said Gabriel to Marceline.

And to Zazie:

'Well? why *do* you want to be one, a teacher?'

'To bitch up the brats,' replied Zazie. 'The ones who'll be my age in ten years, in twenty years, in fifty years, in a hundred years, in a thousand years, always to have kids to beat the hell out of.'

'Well,' said Gabriel.

'I'll be an absolute bastard to them. I'll make them lick the floor. I'll make them eat the blackboard wiper. I'll stick compasses in their behinds. I'll kick their bottoms with my boots. Because I shall wear boots. In the winter. Right up to here (gesture). With great big spurs to pepper their bots with.'

'You know,' said Gabriel calmly, 'if you go by what the papers say, that isn't at all the direction in which modern education is orientated. It's even quite the opposite. The tendency is more towards gentleness, understanding, kindness. Isn't that right, Marceline, that's what it says in the paper?'

'Yes,' replied Marceline gently. 'But Zazie, have they been bullying you at school?'

'Dlike to see them try.'

'In any case,' said Gabriel, 'in twenty years, there won't be any more teachers: they'll be replaced by the cinema, the telly, electronics, things like that. That was in the paper the other day too. Wasn't it, Marceline?'

'Yes,' replied Marceline gently.

Zazie envisaged this future for a moment.

'Well then,' she declared, 'I shall be a space-traveller.'

'Aha,' said Gabriel with approval. 'Aha, have to move with the times.'

'Yes,' continued Zazie, 'I'll be a space-traveller and go and bitch up the Martians.'

Gabriel slapped his sides in his enthusiasm.

'She's full of ideas, this little thing.'

He was delighted.

'She really should go to bed,' said Marceline gently. 'Aren't you tired?'

'No,' replied Zazie, yawning.

'The child's tired,' Marceline went on gently, addressing her remarks to Gabriel, 'she ought to go to bed.'

'You're right,' said Gabriel, and he set to work to concoct an imperative and, if possible, unanswerable sentence.

Before he'd had time to formulate it, Zazie asked him if they had the telly.

'No,' said Gabriel. 'I prefer the cinemascope,' he added insincerely.

'Well then, you could take me to the cinemascope.'

'It's too late,' said Gabriel. 'And anyway, I haven't got time, I start work at eleven.'

'We can do without you,' said Zazie. 'Auntie and I can go by ourselves.'

'I wouldn't like that,' said Gabriel slowly and with a ferocious air.

He stared Zazie straight in the eyes and added nastily:

'Marceline never goes out without me.'

He went on:

'Well, I won't explain, love, it'd take too long.'

Zazie looked away and yawned.

'I'm tired,' she said, 'I'm going to go to bed.'

She got up. Gabriel offered her his cheek. She kissed it.

'What a nice soft skin you've got,' she remarked.

Marceline accompanied her to her room, and Gabriel went to fetch a handsome pigskin manicure set which had his initials stamped on it. He made himself comfortable, poured himself out a large glass of grenadine which he tempered with a little water, and started to do his hands; he adored that, he was very good at it, and preferred himself to any manicurist. He started to hum an obscene song, then, when he'd finished with the prowess of the three goldsmiths, he whistled under his breath, not too loudly, so as not to wake the child, a few olden-day bugle calls, such as lights out, the last post, corporal cuntcuntcount your men, etc.

Marceline comes back.

'It didn't take her long to go to sleep,' she says gently.

She sits down and pours herself out a glass of kirsch.

'A little angel,' comments Gabriel in a neutral voice.

He admires the nail he has just finished, the little finger one, and goes on to the third finger one.

'What on earth are we going to do with her all day?' asks Marceline gently.

'That's no great problem,' says Gabriel. 'To start with I'll take her up to the top of the Eiffel Tower. Tomorrow afternoon.'

'But tomorrow morning?' asks Marceline gently.

Gabriel pales.

'Whatever happens,' says he, 'whatever happens she musn't wake me up.'

'You see,' says Marceline gently. 'A problem.'

Gabriel appeared more and more anguished.

'Children,' he said, 'they get up early in the morning. She's going to stop me sleeping . . . recuperating . . . You know me. I have to recuperate. My ten hours' sleep, they're essential. For my health.'

He looked at Marceline.

'Hadn't you thought of that?'

Marceline lowered her eyes.

'I didn't want to stop you doing your duty,' she said gently.

'Thank you,' said Gabriel in a grave voice. 'But what the bloody hell can we do so's I don't hear her in the morning?'

They started to cogitate.

'We,' said Gabriel, 'could give her a soporific to make her sleep till at least midday or better still till four. It seems there're some marvellous suppositories that do the trick.'

'Knock, knock,' goes Turandot discreetly the other side of the door on the wood of the same.

'Come in,' says Gabriel.

Turandot comes in accompanied by Laverdure. He sits down without waiting to be asked and puts the cage on the table. Laverdure looks at the bottle of grenadine with memorable lust. Marceline pours him out a little in his drinking bowl. Turandot refuses the offer (gesture). Gabriel who has finished his middle finger attacks the first one. With all this going on no one's yet said a word.

Laverdure has golloped down his grenadine. He wipes his beak on his perch, then addresses the meeting as follows:

'Talk, talk, that's all you can do.'

'Talk my arse,' retorts Turandot, provoked.

Gabriel interrupts his labours and looks at the visitor nastily.

'Say that again, eh, what you just said,' says he.

'I said,' says Turandot, 'I said: talk my arse.'

'And what might you be insinuating by that? If I may venture to ask.'

'I'm insinuating about that kid; her being here, I don't like it.'

'Whether you like it or whether youou doowoo no-ot like it, d'you hear me, I don't give a damn.'

'Excuse me. I rented you this place without children and now you've got one without my permission.'

'Your permission, you know what you can do with it?'

'I know, I know, twon't be long now till you start dishonouring me by talking like your niece.'

'It's just not allowed, to be as unintelligent as you are, you know what that means, "unintelligent", you silly bugger?'

'Here we go,' says Turandot, 'any minute now.'

'Talk,' says Laverdure, 'talk, that's all you can do.'

'Any minute now what?' demands Gabriel, distinctly menacing.

'You're already starting to kspress yourself in a repellent fashion.'

'Yknow he's beginning to annoy me,' says Gabriel to Marceline.

'Take it easy,' says Marceline gently.

'I don't want any little sluts in my place,' says Turandot, a pathetic ring in his voice.

'Bugger you,' yells Gabriel. 'You hear me, bugger you.'

He crashes his fist down on the table, which cracks in the usual place. The cage bites the dust, and is followed by the bottle of grenadine, the flask of kirsch, the little glasses, the manicurial apparatus. Laverdure complains brutally, the syrup runs all over the leather goods, Gabriel gives a cry of despair and dives to pick up the polluted object. In doing which he knocks his bloody chair over. A door opens.

'Look here I say hell, isn't anybody allowed to sleep any more?'

Zazie is in her pyjamas. She yawns, and then looks at Laverdure with hostility.

'It's a real menagerie in here,' she declares.

'Talk, talk,' says Laverdure, 'that's all you can do.'

Somewhat taken aback, she neglects the animal for Turandot, apropos of whom she asks her uncle:

'And that chap, who's he?'

Gabriel was wiping the manicure set with a corner of the table cloth.

'Hell,' he murmurs, 'it's had it.'

'I'll buy you another one,' says Marceline gently.

'Oh that's nice,' says Gabriel, 'but in that case I'd rather it wasn't pigskin.'

'What would you like best? Box-calf?'

Gabriel pouts.

'Shagreen?'

Pout.

'Russia leather?'

Pout.

'How about crocodile?'

'That'll be expensive.'

'But it's hard-wearing and smart.'

'All right, I'll go and buy it myself.'

Gabriel, smiling broadly, turned to Zazie.

'You see, your aunt, she's kindness itself.'

'You still haven't told me who that chap is.'

'That's the landlord,' replied Gabriel, 'an exceptional landlord, a pal, and he owns the bistro downstairs.'

'La Cave?'

'Crect,' said Turandot.

'Do you have dancing in your cave?'

'Dancing, no,' said Turandot.

'Pathetic,' said Zazie.

'You don't have to worry about him,' said Gabriel, 'he earns his living very nicely.'

'But at Sangermanndaypray,' said Zazie, 'just think how he'd rake it in, it's in all the papers.'

'It's extremely kind of you to bother your head about my affairs,' said Turandot with a superior air.

'Kind my arse,' retorted Zazie.

Turandot gives a caterwaul of triumph.

'Ha ha,' says he to Gabriel, 'you can't go on saying it's not so, I heard her my arse.'

'Don't talk such obsceneries,' says Gabriel.

'But it isn't me,' says Turandot, 'it's her.'

'He sneaks,' says Zazie. 'That's bad.'

'And anyway I've had enough,' says Gabriel. 'It's time I got going.'

'It can't be much fun being a night watchman,' says Zazie.

'No job is very much fun,' says Gabriel. 'Off you go to bed.'

Turandot picks up the cage and says:

'We'll continue this conversation.'

And he adds, subtly:

'Conversation my arse.'

'Isn't he silly,' says Marceline gently.

'They don't come any sillier.'

'Oh well, good night,' says Turandot, still being amiable, 'I've had a most enjoyable evening, haven't wasted my time.'

'Talk, talk,' says Laverdure, 'that's all you can do.'

'He's sweet,' says Zazie, looking at the animal.

'*Go* to *bed*,' says Gabriel.

Zazie goes out by one door, the visitors by another.

Gabriel waits till everything has calmed down and then goes out himself. He goes down the stairs without making a noise, like a respectable tenant.

But Marceline has seen an object left lying about on a chest of drawers, she picks it up, runs to open the door, leans over the banisters and calls gently:

'Gabriel, Gabriel.'

'What? What is it?'

'You've forgotten your lipstick.'

3

Marceline had fixed up a corner of the room as a sort of recess where Zazie could wash; there was a table, a wash-basin, a water jug, everything just as if it was the backwoods. So that Zazie could feel at home. But Zazie didn't feel at home. She was used to a proper bidet screwed on to the floor and knew, from experience, many other marvels of the sanitary art. Disgusted by this primitivism, she moistened herself slightly, dabbed a little water here and there, and ran her comb once just once through her hair.

She looked into the courtyard; nothing was happening there. In the flat likewise, there seemed to be nothing happening. Her ear stuck to the door, Zazie couldn't perceive any noise. She went out of her room quietly. The livingroomdiningroom was dark and silent. Walking putting one foot down just touching the other like in the game when you're deciding who's to go first, running her fingers over the wall and the furniture and things, it's even more fun when you shut your eyes, she reached the other door which she opened with considerable precaution. This other room was equally dark and silent, someone was peacefully sleeping there. Zazie reshut the door, started walking backwards, which is always fun, and after an extremely long time she came upon a third and other door which she opened with no less considerable precaution than previously. She found herself in the lobby which was illuminated not without difficulty by a window embellished with red and blue panes. One more door to open and Zazie discovers the objective of her excursion: the lav.

As it's the English type, the sort you can sit on, Zazie resumes contact with civilization and spends a good quarter of an hour there. She finds the place not only useful but gay. It's nice and clean, and enamel-painted. The toilet paper scrumples up merrily between your fingers. At this time of day there's even a ray of sunshine: a luminous mist descends from the fanlight. Zazie ponders for a long time, she wonders whether she's going to pull the chain or not. It'll undoubtedly cause chaos to break loose. She hesitates, makes up her mind, pulls, the cataract flows, Zazie waits but nothing seems to have budged, this is the house of the sleeping beauty. Zazie sits down again and tells herself the story in question, inserting close-ups of famous actors as she goes along. She gets a bit carried away by the tale, but, finally, recovering her critical faculties, she finishes by telling herself that fairy tales are a lot of crap and decides to move on.

Back in the lobby, she spies another door which presumably opens on to the landing. Zazie turns the key left in the lock as an illusory precaution, that's what it is all right, and here's Zazie on the landing. She shuts the door behind her very quietly and then very quietly she goes downstairs. She pauses on the first floor; not a sound. Now she's on the ground floor, and here's the passage, the street door is open, a rectangle of light, there we are, Zazie's made it, she's outside.

It's a quiet street. Cars come along it so rarely that you can play hopscotch in the road. There are a few ordinary every-day shops with a provincial look about them. People are walking up and down at a reasonable speed. When they cross, they look first left and then right, combining good citizenship with an excess of prudence. Zazie isn't a hundred percent disappointed, she knows that she is in fact in Paris, that Paris is a big village and that all Paris isn't like this street. Only to verify this and make quite sure of it she'll have to go a bit farther. Which she starts to do, quite happily.

But Turandot suddenly comes out of his bistro and, from the bottom of his steps, he calls to her:

'Hey, Zazie, where d'you think you're going?'

Zazie doesn't answer, she simply walks a bit faster. Turandot climbs up his steps:

'Hey, Zazie,' he calls again and goes on calling.

Zazie immediately breaks into the double. She skims round a corner. The other street is definitely more animated. Zazie is now running at a pretty good lick. No one has the time or takes the trouble to look at her. But Turandot too is going at a good gallop. Running like hell, even. He catches her up, grasps her by the arm and, without a word, firmly turns her round. Zazie doesn't hesitate. She starts yelling:

'Help! Help!'

This cry doesn't fail to attract the attention of the housewives and citizens present. They abandon their personal occupations or unoccupations and interest themselves in the incident.

Given this first rather satisfying result, Zazie redoubles her efforts:

'I don't want to go with the meussieu, I don't know the meussieu, I don't want to go with the meussieu.'

Exetra.

Turandot, sure of the nobility of his cause, ignores these utterances. He soon discovers his mistake when he perceives that he has become the centre of a circle of strict moralists.

In view of this ideal audience, Zazie passes from general considerations to particular, precise, and circumstantial accusations.

'This meussieu,' says she, 'he said dirty things to me.'

'What did he say?' asks a lickerish lady.

'Madame!' exclaims Turandot, 'this little girl has run away from home. I was taking her back to her family.'

The circle guffaws with a scepticism which is already indelible.

The lady wants to hear some more; she leans over towards Zazie.

'It's all right, dear, don't be frightened, tell me what the nasty man said to you.'

'It's too dirty,' murmurs Zazie.

'Did he ask you to do some things to him?'

'That's right, mdame.'

Zazie drops a few whispered details into the ear of the good woman. Who draws herself up and spits in Turandot's face.

'Filthy beast,' she throws at him as well, as a bonus.

And she respits on him again a second time, plonk in the middle of his dial.

A chap enquires:

'What did he ask her to do to him?'

The good woman drops the zazic details in the chap's ear.

'Oh!' says the said chap, 'dnever thought of that one.'

Then he resays, somewhat pensively:

'No, never.'

He turns to another citizen:

'No, really though, just listen to this ... (details). It's unbelievaboo.'

'Certainly are some out and out sods about,' says the other citizen.

Meanwhile the details are being propagated among the crowd. A woman says:

'Don't understand.'

A man explains for her. He takes a bit of paper out of his pocket and makes her a drawing with a ball-point pen.

'Well well,' says the woman dreamily.

'And does it work?'

She's referring to the ball-point pen.

Two enthusiasts are debating:

'Personally,' one of them declares, 'I've heard it said that ... (details).'

'Doesn't surprise me particularly,' retorts the other, 'I've been told that ... (details).'

Impelled from her hovel by curiosity, a shopkeeper's wife indulges in a few confidences:

'Take me for example, my husband, one day, blest if he doesn't take it into his head to ... (details). Where'd he dug that one up, I ask you.'

'Perhaps he'd read a dirty book,' someone suggests.

'He may well have. At any rate, what I did, I told him, my husband that is, you want to? (details). You watch out, I told him. You can go and get yourself stuffed by the wops if you feel like it, but don't bitch me about with your viciousness. That's what I told my husband, who wanted me to ... (details).'

Everyone signifies approval.

Turandot hasn't been listening. He labours under no delusions. Profiting by the technical interest aroused by Zazie's accusations, he has discreetly withdrawn. Hugging the wall he turns the corner and hastily regains the tavern, insinuates himself behind the zinc counter which has been a wooden counter since the occupation, pours himself out a huge glassful of beaujolais which he knocks back at a gulp, and reiterates it. He mops his brow with the thing that serves him for a handkerchief.

Mado Ptits-pieds who is peeling spuds asks him:

'Anything the matter?'

'Don't talk to me about it. Never been in such a funk in my life. They took me for a sex-maniac, all those bleeding clots. If I'd stayed they'd have torn me to shreds.'

'That'll teach you to play the St Bernard,' says Mado Ptits-pieds.

Turandot doesn't answer. He turns on the little telly set that he keeps under his cranium and reviews in his personal news-reel the scene he has just lived through and which has practically caused him to enter the annals if not of history at least of newsitemisation. He shudders as he thinks of the fate he has escaped. Once again the sweat pours down his face.

'Jeezers, jeezers,' he stammers.

'Talk,' says Laverdure, 'talk, that's all you can do.'

Turandot mops himself up, pours himself a third beaujolais.

'Jeezers,' he repeats.

It is the expression which seems to him the most appropriate to the emotion which is disquieting him.

'Oh go on,' says Mado Ptits-pieds, 'you aren't dead.'

'I'd like to have seen you in my shoes.'

'That doesn't mean a thing: "I'd like to have seen you in my shoes." You and me, that's two different things.'

'Oh don't argue, I'm not in the mood.'

'And don't you think they ought to be told upstairs?'

Yes of course, hell, he hadn't thought of that. He abandons his third and still full glass and gets his skates on.

'Goodness,' says Marceline gently, her knitting in her hand.

'The kid,' says Turandot out of breath, 'the kid, eh, well, she's done a bunk.'

Marceline doesn't answer, goes straight to the bedroom. Crect. The kidaskidaddled.

'I saw her,' says Turandot, 'I tried to catch her. Oof! (gesture).'

Marceline goes into Gabriel's room, shakes him, he's heavy, difficult to move, even more so to wake, it's something he likes, sleeping, he snuffles and stirs, when he's asleep he's asleep, you can't shake him out of it as easily as all that.

'What is it,' he finally shouts.

'Zazie's scrammed,' says Marceline gently.

He looks at her. He makes no comment. He gets the hang of things quickly, does Gabriel. He's no fool. He gets up. He goes and has a look round in Zazie's room. He likes to size things up for himself, does Gabriel.

'Perhaps she's locked in the lav,' says he optimistically.

'No,' Marceline answers gently. 'Turandot saw her running away.'

'What *did* you see exactly?' he asks Turandot.

'I saw her running away, so I caught her up and I was trying to bring her back to you.'

'That was nice of you,' says Gabriel, 'you're a real pal.'

'Yes, but she whistled up a crowd round her and she was yelling blue murder that I'd asked her to do this and that to me.'

'And it wasn't true?' asks Gabriel.

'Course it wasn't.'

'You never know.'

'Strew, you never know.'

'You see.'

'Let him go on though,' says Marceline gently.

'Well then, all the people start flocking round me, all ready to break my bloody neck. They took me for a sex maniac, the bleeding apes.'

Gabriel and Marceline laugh like maddening.

'But when I suddenly saw they weren't paying attention to me any more, I scrammed.'

'You'd got the jitters?'

'And how. Never been in such a funk in all my life. Even during the bombing.'

'Oh,' says Gabriel, 'I was never scared in the raids. Seeing that it was the English, I reckoned that their bombs weren't for me but for the Jerries, since I was waiting for them with open arms, the English.'

'That was a damn silly way of thinking,' Turandot points out.

'All the same I never was afraid and I never even got the slightest scratch, you know, even during the worst ones. But the Fritzes, talk about the squitters, they were tearing into the shelters, couldn't see them for dust, all I did was laugh, I stayed outside watching the fireworks, smacko bang in the middle, up goes a munitions dump, the station's pulverized, the factory's smashed to smithereens, the town's in flames, a marvellous sight.'

Gabriel concludes and sighs:

'After all it wasn't such a bad life.'

'Far as I was concerned,' says Turandot, 'in the war, I had nothing to write home about. With the black market, I behaved like a perfect fool. I don't know how I did it, but I was always collecting fines, they swiped my stuff, the state, the tax bods, the controls, they closed my shop down, in June 44 I'd got a little bit of lolly tucked away but only just, and just as well at that because at that very moment a bomb arrives and that's it. Cleaned out. Luckily I inherited this dump, otherwise.'

'You haven't really got anything to grumble at, when you come down to it,' says Gabriel, 'you've got it dead easy, it's a cushy job, your trade.'

'I'd like to see you at it. It's back-breaking, my trade, back-breaking, and bad for your health into the bargain.'

'Then what would you say if you had to work at night like me. And sleep in the daytime. Sleeping in the daytime is exceedingly tiring, though you mightn't think so. And I'm not talking about when you get woken up at an impossible hour like today ... I shouldn't like it to be like that every morning.'

'Lhave to lock her in, that girl,' says Turandot.

'I wonder why she ran away,' murmurs Gabriel pensively.

'She didn't want to make a noise,' says Marceline gently, 'and so as not to wake you she went for a walk.'

'But I don't want her to go for walks by herself,' says Gabriel, 'the street is the school of vice, everyone knows that.'

'Maybe it's what the papers call a case of phobia,' says Turandot.

'That wouldn't be very funny,' says Gabriel, 'have to call in the rozzers, prolly. And what'd I look like then?'

'Don't you think,' says Marceline gently, 'that you ought to try and find her?'

'Far as I'm concerned,' says Gabriel, 'I'm going back to bed.'

He orientates himself in the direction of the downy.

'It's no more than your duty, to retrieve her,' says Turandot.

Gabriel cackles. He simpers, and imitating Zazie's voice:

'Duty my arse,' declares he.

He adds:

'She'll find herself quite well by herself.'

'Supposing,' says Marceline gently, 'supposing she comes across a sex-maniac?'

'Like Turandot?' asks Gabriel facetiously.

'I don't think that's funny,' says Turandot.

'Gabriel,' says Marceline gently, 'you ought to make a little effort to get her back.'

'You go.'

'I've got my washing on the boil.'

'You ought to take your laundry to those automatic American whatsits,' says Turandot to Marceline, 'it'd make less work for you, that's what I do.'

'And,' says Gabriel cunningly, 'what if she enjoys doing her own washing? Eh? What's it got to do with you? talk, talk, that's all you can do. Your American whatsits, you know where you can put 'em.'

And he gives himself a tap on the behind.

'Well well,' says Turandot ironically, 'and there was me thinking you were an americanophile.'

'Americanophile!' ksclaims Gabriel, 'you use words you don't even know the meaning of. Americanophile! as if that stopped people washing their dirty linen at home. Marceline and I, not only are we americanophiles, but over and above that, little man, and at the same time, do you hear, little man, AT THE SAME TIME, we are washingophiles. Eh? that stumps you, doesn't it (pause) little man.'

Turandot can't find an answer. He comes back to the concrete and present problem, to the hick 'n nunk, the one it isn't so easy to wash your hands of.

'You ought to go after that child,' he advises Gabriel.

'So that the same thing can happen to me that happened to you? so that I can get myself linenched by the common Hurd?'

Turandot shrugs his shoulders.

'You too,' says he scornfully, 'talk, talk, that's all you can do.'

'Do go,' says Marceline gently to Gabriel.

'You make me sick, both of you,' grumbled Gabriel.

He goes back to his room, dresses methodically, passes his hand sadly over his chin which he hasn't had time to epilate, sighs, reappears.

Turandot and Marceline or rather Marceline and Turandot are debating the merits or demerits of washing machines. Gabriel kisses Marceline on the forehead.

'Adieu,' says he gravely, 'I go to do my duty.'

He shakes Turandot's hand vigorously; the emotion to which he is a prey allows him to pronounce no other historical dictum than: 'I go to do my duty', but his gaze becomes veiled with the melancholy appropriate to those individuals whom a glorious destiny awaits.

The others fall into meditation.

He goes. He is gone.

Outside he sniffs the air. He can only smell the usual scents, and in particular those which emanate from La Cave. He doesn't know whether he should go north or south, for the road is thus orientated. But a vocal summons transvects his hesitations. It is Gridoux, the shoemaker, who is calling him from his workshop. Gabriel goes over.

'You're looking for the little girl, I'll bet.'

'Yes,' grunts Gabriel without enthusiasm.

'I know where she's gone.'

'You always know everything,' says Gabriel with some ill-humour.

This fellow, says he to himself with his still small inner voice, every time I pass the time of day with him he egzaggerates my complex inferiority.

'Aren't you interested?' asks Gridoux.

'I'm obliged to be interested.'

'Ltell you then, shall I?'

'They're a funny lot, cobblers,' replies Gabriel, 'they never stop working, you'd think they like it, and to show that they never stop they put themselves in a shopwindow so's people can admire them. Like the girls who mend stockings.'

'And what about you?' retorts Gridoux, 'what do *you* put yourself in so's people can admire you?'

Gabriel scratches his head.

'In nothing,' he says feebly, 'I'm a nartist. I don't do any harm. And anyway this isn't the moment to talk that sort of stuff to me, this business of the brat is urgent.'

'I talk about it because I enjoy talking about it,' replies Gridoux calmly.

He lifts up his nose from his work.

'Well,' asks he, 'bloody gabber, do you want to know or don't you?'

'I tell you it's urgent.'

Gridoux smiles.

'Did Turandot tell you the start of it?'

'He told me what he felt like telling me.'

'In any case, what you're interested in is what happened next.'

'Yes,' says Gabriel, 'what happened next?'

'Next? Isn't the beginning enough for you? It's a case of phobia with that youngster. A phobia!'

'That's cheerful,' murmured Gabriel.

'All you have to do is tell the police.'

'That doesn't appeal to me,' says Gabriel in a much enfeebled voice.

'She won't come back of her own accord.'

'You never know.'

Gridoux shrugged his shoulders.

'After all, what I say, I don't give a damn.'

'No more do I,' says Gabriel, 'fundamentally.'

'*Have* you got a fundament?'

It was Gabriel's turn to shrug his shoulders. If this fellow was going to start being insolent into the bargain. Without another word he went back home to bed.

4

Seeing that her fellow-countrymen and -women were all set to continue the cuntroversy, Zazie scrammed. She took the first street to the right, then the ditto to the left, and so on until she arrived at the outskirts of the town. Superb skyscrapers four or five storeys high lined a sumptuous avenue on the pavement of which verminous street-stalls were jostling one another. A thick mauve crowd was trickling in from all sides. A woman selling monster balloons, and the music coming from the roundabouts added their chaste note to the virulence of the show. Zazie was lost in admiration, and it was some time before she noticed at no great distance from her a masterpiece of baroque ironmongery growing out of the pavement which was crowned with the inscription METRO. Immediately forgetting the pleasures of the street, Zazie approached its mouth, her own dry with emotion. Working her way with tiny steps round the outside railing, she at last discovered the entrance. But the iron gate was shut. A pendent slate bore a chalk inscription which Zazie deciphered without difficulty. The strike was still on. A smell of ferruginous and dehydrated dust rose gently from the forbidden depths. Heartbroken, Zazie began to cry.

This gave her such keen pleasure that she went and sat down on a bench, in order to snivel in greater comfort. After a short time, though, she was distracted from her grief by the perception of a neighbouring presence. She waited with curiosity to see what would happen next. What happened next took the form of words uttered by a masculine voice in falsetto, these words forming the interrogative sentence that follows:

'Come, my child, are you really so unhappy?'

In the face of the stupid hypocrisy of this question, Zazie redoubled the volume of her tears. So many sobs seemed to be crowding into her chest that she appeared not to have time to suppress them all.

'Is it as bad as all that?' he asked.

'Oh yess, msieu.'

It was definitely time to see what sort of a mug the sex-maniac had. Smearing her face with a hand that transformed the torrents of tears into muddy grooves, Zazie turned and looked at the chap. She couldn't believe her eyes. He was rigged out with an enormous handle-bar moustache, a bowler, a brolly, and huge beetle-crushers. Snot possible, said Zazie to herself with her little inner voice, snot possible, he's an actor from ye olden days, a Strolling Player. She even forgot to laugh.

The individual pulled a pleasant sort of face and offered the child a handkerchief of astonishing cleanliness. Zazie seized it and deposited in it a little of the humid filth which was stagnating on her cheeks, and complemented this offering with a copious portion of snot.

'Come on now,' said the chap in encouraging tones, 'what's the matter? Do your parents beat you? Or is it that you've lost something and you're afraid they'll be cross with you?'

He was full of theories. Zazie gave him back his handkerchief, much moistened. He displayed no sign of disgust as he put this muck back in his kick. He went on:

'Better tell me all about it. Don't be afraid. You can trust me.'

'Why?' mumbled Zazie slyly.

'Why?' repeated the chap, disconcerted.

He started raking the asphalt with his brolly.

'Yes,' said Zazie, 'why should I trust you?'

'Why,' replied the chap, stopping scratching the ground, 'because I like children. Little girls. And little boys.'

'You're a dirty old man, that's what you are.'

'Certainly not,' declared the chap with a vehemence that astonished Zazie.

Taking advantage of this point scored, the meussieu offered her a cacocalo, over there, at the nearest café, it being fully understood, natch: in broad daylight, in full view of everybody, a perfectly respectable proposition, what.

Not wishing to betray her enthusiasm at the idea of getting outside a cacocalo, Zazie fell to a solemn contemplation of the crowd which, on the other side of the road, was flowing in between two rows of stalls.

'What are all those people doing?' she asked.

'They're going to the flea market,' said the chap, 'or rather it's the flea market that's going to them, because it starts there.'

'Ah, the flea market,' said Zazie, looking like people do when they're determined not to be impressed, 'that's where you discover rembrants going cheap, then afterwards you sell them to a Yank and you haven't wasted your time.'

'There's not only rembrants,' said the chap, 'there's cork soles too, and lavender, and nails, and even jackets that haven't been worn.'

'Do they have American surplus too?'

'Course they do. And stalls where you can buy chips too. Good ones. Made the same morning.'

'American surplus things are fabulous.'

'For people that want them, there's even mussels. Good ones. That don't poison you.'

'D'they have blewgenes in their American surplus stalls?'

'Natchrally they do. And compasses which work in the dark.'

'Don't give a damn about compasses,' said Zazie. 'But blewgenes (silence).'

'We can go and look,' said the chap.

'And then what?' said Zazie. 'I haven't got a bean to buy them with. Unless I whip a pair.'

'Let's go and look just the same,' said the chap.

Zazie had finished her cacocalo. She looked at the chap and said: 'I can see you coming a mile off.'

She added:

'Shall we go?'

The chap pays and they immerse themselves in the crowd. Zazie winds in and out, neglecting the engravers of name-plates for bicycles, the glass-blowers, the demonstrators of bow-ties, the Arabs offering watches, the Romanies offering more or less anything. The chap's at her heels, he's as artful as Zazie. For the moment she has no desire to shake him off, but she tells herself in advance that it won't be so easy. No doubt about it, he's a specialist.

She stopped dead in front of a display of surplus. What a sight; she doesn't budge. She doesn't budget all. The chap steps on his brakes, just behind her. The stallholder initiates the conversation.

'Is it the compass you fancy?' he asks coolly. 'The electric torch? the rubber dinghy?'

Zazie is trembling with desire and anxiety, because she isn't at all sure that the chap really has got dishonourable intentions. She dares not articulate the disyllabic and anglo-saxon word which would mean what she means. It's the chap who pronounces it.

'You wouldn't by any chance have a pair of blewgenes for the little girl?' he asks the middleman. 'That *is* what you'd like?'

'Oh yess,' yespers Zazie.

'A pair of blewgenes, by any chance?' says the flea-marketeer. 'I should think I have indeed. I've even got some which are positively impossible to wear out.'

'Yerss,' says the chap, 'but you can well imagine that she hasn't stopped growing yet. By next year she won't be able to get the things on, and what'll we do with them then?'

'They'll do for her little brother or her little sister.'

'Hasn't got any.'

'A year from now she might have (laugh).'

'It's no joking matter,' says the chap lugubriously, 'her poor mother's dead.'

'Oh! beg yours.'

Zazie looks at the sex-maniac with curiosity for a moment, with interest, even, but these are asides to go into later on. Inwardly she's itching all over, she can't stand it any longer, she asks:

'Have you got my size?'

'Certainly, mademoiselle,' replies the stall-keeper with old-world courtesy.

'And how much are they?'

It's still Zazie who's asked this question. Automatically. Because she's economical but not mean. The other says how much they cost. The chap nods. He doesn't seem to think that's so very dear. At least that's what Zazie concludes from his behaviour.

'Could I try them on?' she asks.

The bazaarist is staggered: the little clotface seems to think she's at Fior's. He gives a pretty smile with all his teeth and says:

'No need to bother. Just have a look at this.'

He unfolds the garment and holds it up in front of her. Zazie pouts. She'd have liked to try them on.

'Won't they be too big?' she asks.

'Look! They won't come down further than the calf, and just have a look how narrow they are, tll be a near thing if you can get into them at all, mademoiselle, though you are very slim, to say the least.'

Zazie's throat is quite dry. Blewgenes. Oy oy oy. For her first parisian outing. That'd be super-smashing.

Suddenly the chap gets that far away look. Seems as if he isn't thinking about what's going on around him any more.

The stallholder gets to work again.

'You won't regret it, believe me,' he goes on, 'you can't wear them out, positively unwearoutable.'

'I've already told you I don't give a damn if they're unwearoutable,' answers the chap absent-mindedly.

'All the same it's quite a point, unwearoutability,' insists the salesman.

'But,' says the chap suddenly, 'after all, by the way, it would appear, if I understand aright, that these are American surplus, these blewgenes?'

'Natürlich,' answers the stallholder.

'Well then, perhaps you can explain this one; did they have baby dolls in their army, the Yanks?'

'They had something of everything,' replies the stall-holder, not disconcerted.

The chap doesn't seem convinced.

'Oh well you know,' says the middleman who has no desire to

37

miss a sale on account of world history, 'takes all sorts to make a war.'

'And these?' asks the chap, 'how much are these?'

These are antisunglasses. He dresses up in them.

'They're a bonus for everyone who buys a pair of blewgenes,' says the pedlar who sees it's in the bag.

Zazie znot so sure. Oh hell, can't he make up his mind? What's he waiting for? What does he think? What does he want? There's certainly something sordid about him, he's not one of those chaps that are disgusting but you can easily frighten off, this one's a really sordid bozo. Gottabe careful, gottabe careful, gottabe careful. But hell, blewgenes . . .

At last the deal is concluded. He pays for them. The merchandise is wrapped up and the chap puts the parcel under his arm. *His* arm. Zazie, inwardly, really starts to create. So it isn't over yet?

'And now,' says the chap, 'we'll go and have a bite to eat.'

He walks in front, self-confidence personified. Zazie follows, squinting at the parcel. He leads her thus to a café-restaurant. They sit down. The parcel gets put on a chair, out of Zazie's reach.

'What'd you like?' asks the chap. 'Mussels or chips?'

'Both,' replies Zazie, who can feel herself going mad with rage.

'Well, bring some mussels for the little girl, anyway,' says the chap calmly to the waitress. 'I'll have a muscadet with two lumps of sugar.'

While they're waiting for the grub they don't speak. The chap is peacefully smoking. When the mussels are served Zazie throws herself on them, submerges herself in the sauce, splashes in the juice, smudges herself all over. The lamellibranchia that have resisted the process of cooking are forced out of their shells with merovingian ferocity. She all but bites open the shells. When she's liquidated the lot, well yes, she doesn't mind if she does have some chips. Right, says the chap. He's sipping his mixture in little gulps, as if it were hot chartreuse. The chips are brought. They're boiling hot for a change. The voracious Zazie burns her fingers but not her tongue.

When they're all gone she knocks back her shandy at one gulp, lets out three little belches and slumps down on her chair, worn out. Her face, over which quasi-anthropophagical shadows have been passing, brightens. She's thinking with some satisfaction that at least that's something that can't be taken away from her. Then she wonders if it mightn't be time to say something pleasant to the chap, but what? With a big effort she thinks this up:

'You certainly take your time, swigging it back. My papa now, he would have sunk ten like that in that time.'

'Does he drink a lot, your papa?'

'Did he drink, you should say. He's dead.'

'Were you very sad when he died?'

'Not a chance (gesture). Didn't have time with all that was going on (silence).'

'And what *was* going on?'

'I could do with another half-pint, but not a shandy, a real half-pint of real beer.'

The chap orders for her and asks for a small spoon. He wants to salvage the remains of the sugar in the bottom of his glass. While he is giving himself up to this operation, Zazie licks the froth off her beer, then replies:

'Do you read the papers?'

'Now and then.'

'D'you remember about the dressmaker from Saint-Montron who split open her husband's skull with a chopper? Well, that was my mamma. And the husband, naturally enough, was my papa.'

'Ah!' says the chap.

'Don't you remember?'

He doesn't seem too sure. Zazie is indignant.

'Hell, it made enough stink though. My mamma had a lawyer that came from Paris specially for her, a famous one, one who doesn't talk like you and me, a twerp, eh. Didn't stop him getting her acquitted, though, just like that (gesture), as easy as picking your nose. And the people clapped her, my mamma, next thing you knew they'd have carried her through the streets in triumph. What a party we had that day. There was only one thing that worried Mamma though, that was that the Parisian, the lawyer, it wasn't chicken-feed, what he wanted, when it came to paying his bill. A really greedy type, the swine. Lucky that Georges was there for once.'

'And who was this Georges?'

'A pork-butcher. All pink. Mamma's loved-one. He was the one who slipped her the axe (silence) to chop up the wood (little laugh).'

She despatches a little gulp of beer with an air of distinction, next thing you know she'll be curling up her little finger.

'And that's not all there is to it,' she adds, 'I, the very same person you see before you, well, I gave evidence at the trial, and in camera what's more.'

The chap doesn't react.

'Don't you believe me?'

'Course I don't. It's not legal, a child that gives evidence against its parents.'

'In the first place, parents, there was only one left, primo, and in the next place you don't know what you're talking about. You just come and see us at Saint-Montron and I'll show you an exercise book where I've stuck all the newspaper articles where there's something about me. Yes and Georges, while Mamma was in jug, for my Christmas present, he even gave me a subscription to the *Argus de la Presse*. Do you know it, the *Argus de la Presse*?'

'No,' says the chap.

'Pathetic. And yet he tries to argue with me.'

'Why should you give evidence in camera?'

'You *are* interested, then?'

'Not specially.'

'No one can say you're not artful.'

And she despatches a little gulp of beer with an air of distinction, next thing you know she'll be curling up her little finger. The chap doesn't turn a hair (silence).

'Come on,' says Zazie finally, 'no need to sulk. I'll tell you my story.'

'I'm listening.'

'Right. First thing you have to know is that Mamma couldn't stomach Papa, so Papa, that'd made him sad, and he'd taken to the booze. Couldn't he just knock it back. Well, when he was like that, had to get out of his way, even the cat would have been for it. Like in the song. You know it?'

'I see,' says the chap.

'Just as well. Then I'll go on: one day, a Sunday, I'd come back from watching a football match, it was the Sanctimontronians v. the Red Star of Neuflize, in the first division, that's quite something. You interested in sport?'

'Yes. Wrestling.'

Considering the modest dimensions of the individual, Zazie cackles.

'On the spectators' side,' says she.

'That's a chestnut,' retorts the chap coldly.

Zazie swigs back her beer in fury, then she shuts her trap.

'Come on,' says the chap, 'no need to sulk. Go on with your story.'

'So you're interested in my story?'

'Yes.'

'Well then, you were lying just now?'

'Oh get on with it.'

'Don't get excited. You wouldn't be in a fit state to appreciate my story.'

5

The chapshutistrap and Zazie resumed the conversation in these terms:

'So he was all by himself at home, then, my old man, he was waiting all by himself, he wasn't waiting for anything special, he was just waiting, and he was all by himself, that's to say he thought he was all by himself, hang on a minute and you'll see what it's all about. I get home, then, and there he was boozed as a coot, my papa, so he starts to kiss me which was quite natural seeing he was my papa, but then he starts pawing me (wolf whistle), so I say oh no you don't because I could see what he was getting at, the bastard, but when I'd said ah no, not that, never, he flings himself on to the door and he locks it and he puts the key in his pocket and he rolls his eyes and he goes aha just like they do in the movies, it was terrific. You've got it coming, he kept shouting, you've got it coming, he was even frothing at the mouth a bit as he uttered these unspeakable menaces, and finally he pounced on me. It was dead easy to dodge him. He was plastered and so he fell flat on his face. He gets up again, he starts chasing me again, to make a long story short, a real bull-fight. And then, here, he finally catches me. And the pawing (wolf whistle) starts all over again. But at this moment the door starts to open, quiet as you like, because what had happened, my mamma'd told him, casually you know, I'm going out, I'm going to buy some spaghetti and some pork chops, but it wasn't true, she was just having him on, she'd gone to ground in the wash house, that's where she'd parked the chopper, and she'd crep back quiet as a mouse, and naturally she'd got her keys on her. No fool, the old girl, eh?'

'Well, yes,' says the chap.

'Right then, she opens the door, quiet as can be, and comes in minding her own business, my papa he had his mind on other things the poor sodder, he wasn't paying attention you might say, and that's how he got his skull split open. You have to hand it to her, she made a good job of it, my mamma. It wasn't a pretty sight. Nauseating, even. Enough to give me no end of complexes. And that's how she was acquitted. It wasn't any use my saying that it was Georges who'd slipped her the chopper, didn't make any difference, they said that when you have a husband that's a bastard of that magnitude, zonly one thing you can do and that's rub him out. Iyalready told you, they even congratulated her. That's just about the end, don't you think?'

'People . . .' says the chap (gesture).

'Afterwards she told me off like anything: you silly bitch, she said, what did you want to go and tell them all that about the chopper for? Well hell, I replied, wasn't it the truth? Silly bitch, she repeated, and she was going to beat the hell out of me, in the general rejoicing. But Georges calmed her down and anyway she was so proud of having gone down so good with people she didn't even know that she couldn't think about anything else any more. For a time, at any rate.'

'And then what?' asked the chap.

'Oh well then it was Georges who started making passes at me. So Mamma just said that well really she couldn't kill the lot of them, it would begin to look a bit funny, so she slung him out, she deprived herself of her loved-one for my sake. Don't you think that's decent? Don't you think she's a good mother?'

'Well, yes,' says the chap, non-committally.

'Only not long ago she found herself another one and that's what brought her to Paris, she's chasing him, but then there was me, and so's not to leave me alone a prey to all the sex-maniacs, and there's bags of 'em about, just bags of 'em, she got my Unkoo Gabriel to look after me. It seems that with him I've nothing to be afraid of.'

'Why not?'

'That I don't know. I only got here yesterday and I haven't had time to find out.'

'And what does he do, your Uncle Gabriel?'

'He's a night-watchman, he never gets up before twelve, one o'clock.'

'And you sneaked off while he was still snoozing.'

'Sit.'

'And where do you live?'

'Thataway (gesture).'

'And why were you crying just now on the bench?'

Zazie doesn't answer. This chap, he's starting to get on her wick.

'You're lost, eh?'

Zazie shrugs her shoulders. He really is a stinker.

'Could you tell me your Uncle Gabriel's address?'

Zazie and her little inner voice are addressing each other at length: no but what am I letting myself in for, what's his idea, you can't say he hasn't asked for what he's going to get.

All of a sudden she gets up, snatches the parcel and scrams. She flings herself into the crowd, worms her way along in between the people and the stalls, goes full speed ahead in a zigzag, then turns abruptly sometimes to the right, sometimes to the left, she runs and then she walks, she hurries and then she slows down, she resumes a gentle trot, with much twisting and turning.

She was just going to have a good laugh at the poor boob and how sick he must be looking when she realised that she was congratulating herself too soon. Someone was walking by her side. No need to raise her eyes to know that it was the chap, nevertheless she did raise them, you never know, it could be another chap, but no it was the same one all right, he didn't look as if he thought anything unusual had been happening, he was just walking along in an ordinary sort of way, minding his own business.

Zazie said nothing. With a surreptitious glance she egzamined the vicinity. They had emerged from the crowd, they were now in a street of moderate width which was frequented by decent people with silly buggers' faces, paterfamiliasses, old-age pensioners, mums taking their brats for a walk, the salt of the earth, eh. It's child's play, said Zazie to herself with her little inner voice. She took a breath and opened her mouth to utter her battle cry: help! a sex-maniac!

But the chap wasn't born yesterday. Maliciously snatching the parcel from her he started shaking her, energetically pronouncing the following words:

'Aren't you ashamed of yourself, you little thief, while I'd got my back turned.'

He then appealed to the gathering crowd:

'Ah! the post-war generation, just have a look what she tried to pinch from me.'

And he waved the parcel about over his head.

'A pair of blewgenes,' he yelled. 'A pair of blewgenes she tried to pinch from me, this little creature did.'

'Oh what a shame,' comments a housewife.

'Rotten stock,' says another.

'The scum of the earth,' says a third, 'hasn't anyone ever taught this child that property is sacred, then?'

The chap carried on carrying on at the brat.

'Eh? and what if I took you to the station? Eh? To the police station? You'd go to prison. To prison. And you'd come up before the juvenile court. And the result would be a reformatory. Because you'd be convicted. Convicted and given the maximum sentence.'

A society lady who happened to be passing these parts on her way to pick up some rare curios deigned to stop. She made enquiries of the populace as to the cause of the disturbance and when, not without difficulty, she had understood, she felt the desire to appeal to the humane sentiments which it was possible might exist in this singular individual, whose bowler, black handle-bars and dark glasses did not seem to astonish the population.

'Meussieu,' she said, 'have pity on this child. She is not responsible for the poor education which, perhaps, she has received. Hunger, probably, impelled her to commit this evil action, but one must not reproach her too much, and I mean "too much". Have you never been hungry (silence), meussieu?'

'I, madame,' replied the chap bitterly (they couldn't do it any better on the movies, said Zazie to herself), 'I? been hungry? But I was brought up on Public Assistance, madame . . .'

The crowd caused itself to vibrate with a murmur of compassion.

The chap, taking advantage of the effect produced, elbows his way through it, this crowd, with Zazie in tow, declaiming in the grand manner: 'we shall soon see what your parents will say.'

Then a bit further on he shut up. They walked in silence for a few moments and, all of a sudden, the chap said:

'Goodness me, I've left my brolly in the bistro.'

He was talking to himself and under his breath at that, but it didn't take Zazie long to draw certain conclusions from this remark. He wasn't a sex-maniac disguised as a bogus cop, but a real cop disguised as a bogus sex-maniac disguised as a real cop. The proof of this was that he'd forgotten his brolly. As this line of argument seemed to her to be incontestable, Zazie wondered whether it wouldn't be a smashing trick to confront her unkoo with a cop, a real one. Consequently, when the chap said well now, to come down to brass tacks, where was it she lived, she gave him the address without hesitation. The trick did in fact turn out to be smashing: when Gabriel, having opened the door and exclaimed Zazie, heard it gayly announced 'unkoo, this is a cop and he wants to talk to you,' propping himself up against the wall he turned green. It's true that this could have been the effect of the light, it was so dark in that lobby, in any case the chap adopted the attitude of not having noticed anything, Gabriel said to him just like that come in then in a wobbly sort of voice.

So they went into the dining room and Marceline threw herself upon Zazie displaying the greatest joy at having found the child again. Gabriel said: well, ask the meussieu if he'd like a drink, but the other intimated that he had no desire to ingurgitate anything, which wasn't the case with Gabriel who asked for the bottle of grenadine.

Without waiting to be asked the chap had sat down, while Gabriel poured himself out a generous helping of the syrup which he embellished with a little water.

'Won't you really have anything to drink?'

'(gesture)'

Gabriel knocked back his pick-me-up, put the glass on the table and waited, looking into the middle distance, but the chap didn't seem to be feeling chatty. Zazie and Marceline, standing up, observed them.

This could have gone on a long time.

Finally Gabriel found a way of getting the conversation going.

'Well then,' he said casually, 'well then so you're a cop?'

'Not on your life,' exclaimed the other cordially, 'I am nothing but a poor street-vendor.'

'Don't you believe him,' said Zazie, 'he's a poor cop.'

'Make your minds up,' said Gabriel feebly.

'The little girl's joking,' said the chap with unshaken good humour. 'I go by the name of Pedro-surplus, and you can find me at the Flea Market on Saturdays, Sundays and Mondays, distributing to the populace the petty objects scattered in their wake by the Amerrigan army at the time of the liberation of the territory.'

'And do you distribute them free?' asked Gabriel, vaguely interested.

'You're joking,' said the chap. 'I exchange them for petty cash (silence). Except in the present instance.'

'What d'you mean?' asked Gabriel.

'I simply mean that this child (gesture) pinched a pair of blewgenes from me.'

'If that's all it is,' said Gabriel, 'she'll give them back to you.'

'The bastard,' said Zazie, 'he's taken them back.'

'Well then,' said Gabriel to the chap, 'what're you grumbling at?'

'I'm just grumbling, that's all.'

'They're mine, the blewgenes,' said Zazie. 'It was him that pinched them from me. Yes. And what's more, he's a cop. You want to watch out, Unkoo Gabriel.'

Gabriel, not at his ease, poured himself out another glass of grenadine.

'It's a bit fishy, all this,' says he. 'If you're a cop I can't see why you're moaning, and if you aren't one, there's no reason for you to be asking me questions.'

'Excuse me,' said the chap, 'it's not me that's asking questions, it's you.'

'Yes, that's true,' Gabriel acknowledged, with objectivity.

'That's done it,' said Zazie, 'he's a gone gosling.'

'Perhaps it's my turn to ask questions now,' said the chap.

'Don't say a word till your lawyer gets here,' said Zazie.

'You shut your big mouth,' said Gabriel. 'I know what I have to do.'

'He'll make you say anything he likes.'

'She takes me for an idiot,' said Gabriel amiably to the chap. 'That's the modern child for you.'

'No respect for their elders any more,' said the chap.

'It's nauseating to have to listen to such crap,' declares Zazie, who's had an idea. 'I'm off.'

'That's right,' says the chap. 'If the members of the second sex could retire for a moment.'

'Only too pleased,' says Zazie, cackling.

As she left the room she discreetly retrieved the parcel which the chap had put down on a chair and forgotten.

'We'll leave you, then,' says Marceline gently, also beating it.

She shuts the door gently behind her.

'Well then,' says the chap, '(silence) and so that's how you make your living, prostituting little girls.'

Gabriel makes as if to rise in a gesture of theatrical protest, but immediately shrivels up.

'*I* do, msieu?' he murmurs.

'Yes!' retorts the chap, 'yes, you. You aren't going to say you don't?'

'Yes I am, msieu.'

'Well you've got a nerve. Caught in the act. That child was soliciting in the flea market. I hope at least that you don't sell her to the Arabs?'

'No, never that, msieu.'

'Nor to the Poles?'

'Nor to them either, msieu.'

'Only to the French and to tourists of substance?'

'Only nothing at all.'

The grenadine was starting to work. Gabriel was recovering.

'So you deny it?' asks the chap.

'And how.'

The chap smiles diabolically, like in the movies.

'And tell me, my good man,' he murmurs, 'what is the trade or profession behind which you dissemble your felonious activities?'

'I tell you I haven't got any felonious activities.'

'Come off it. Profession?'

'Artist.'

'You? an artist? The girl told me you were a night-watchman.'

'She doesn't know anything about it. Anyway people don't always tell the truth to children. Do they?'

'They do to me.'

'But you aren't a child (pleasant smile). A grenadine?'

'(gesture).'

Gabriel helps himself to another glass of grenadine.

'Well,' the chap goes on, 'what kind of artist?'

Gabriel lowers his eyes modestly.

'Ballerina,' he replies.

6

'What are they saying?' asked Zazie, doing up the blewgenes.

'They're talking too quietly,' said Marceline, gently, her ear against the door. 'I can't hear properly.'

She was gently lying, was Marceline, because she could very clearly hear the chap who was saying as follows: 'So that's the reason, because you're a queer, that the mother asked you to look after this child?' and Gabriel was answering: 'But I tell you I'm not one. All right, yes, I do an act dressed up as a woman in a fairies' night club but that doesn't mean a thing. It's just to make people laugh. You see, because I'm so tall they split their sides. But me personally, I'm not one. Stands to reason since I'm married.'

Zazie was looking at herself in the mirror and drooling with admiration. Talk about suiting her yes you certainly could say the blewgenes suited her. She ran her hands over her little buttocks which they fitted like a cross between a glove and a dream, and sighed profoundly, completely satisfied.

'Can't you really hear anything?' she asks. 'Nothing at all?'

'No,' replied Marceline gently, still equally mendacious because the chap was saying: 'Doesn't mean a thing. In any case you can't deny that it's because the mother considers you're as good as a fairy that she left you in charge of the child;' and Gabriel had to agree. 'There's something in that, there's something in that,' he admitted.

'How d'you like me?' Zazie asked. 'Aren't they fabulous?'

Marceline stopped listening and observed her.

'That's how girls dress nowadays,' she said gently.

'Don't you like it?'

'Of course I do. But tell me, are you sure that the fellow won't say anything about your taking his parcel?'

'I tell you they're mine. Won't he look sick when he sees me with them on.'

'Because you're thinking of showing yourself before he's gone?'

'Certainly am,' said Zazie. 'I'm not going to stay and rot here.'

She crossed the room and went and stuck an ear against the door. She heard the chap saying: 'Huh, where'd I put my parcel?'

'Hey Auntie Marceline,' said Zazie, 'are you having me on or are you really hard of hearing? You can hear what they're saying perfectly well.'

'Well, what *are* they saying?'

Temporarily renouncing the idea of an enquiry into the question of the possible deafness of her aunt, Zazie again thrust her ear against the wood of the door. The chap was saying as follows: 'Huh, half a mo, hope that child hasn't whipped my parcel.' And Gabriel was suggesting: 'perhaps you didn't have it with you.' 'Oh yes I did,' the chap was saying, 'if that brat has whipped it there's going to be trouble.'

'Doesn't he go on,' said Zazie.

'Isn't he going?' asked Marceline gently.

'No,' said Zazie. 'Now he's tackling uncle about you.'

After all, the chap was saying, perhaps it was your missis who whipped it, my parcel that is. Maybe she wants to wear blewgenes too, your missis. No question of that, Gabriel was saying, none at all. How do you know? the chap was retorting, the idea might have come into her head with a husband who acts like a hormosessual.

'What's that, a hormosessual?' Zazie asked.

'It's a man who wears blewgenes,' said Marceline gently.

'You're pulling my leg,' said Zazie.

'Gabriel ought to throw him out,' said Marceline gently.

'Now that's a beautiful idea,' Zazie said.

Then sceptical:

'Would he have the guts to?'

'You'll see.'

'Hang on, I'll go in first.'

She opened the door and, in a loud, clear voice, pronounced the following words:

'Well, Uncle Gabriel, how d'you like my blewgenes?'

'Take them off at once, will you,' cried Gabriel, appalled, 'and give them back to the meussieu this minute.'

'Give them back my arse,' declared Zazie. 'Zno reason to. They're mine.'

'I'm not so sure,' said Gabriel, annoyed.

'Yes,' said the chap, 'take 'em off and that sharpish.'

'Oh, sling him out,' said Zazie to Gabriel.

'You're certainly full of good ideas,' said Gabriel. 'You inform me that he's a cop and then you want me to beat him up.'

'Just because he's a cop's no reason to be afraid of him,' said Zazie grandiloquently. 'He za dirty old man and he made improper advances to me, so we'll take him to court, copper or no copper, and the judges, I know all about judges, they like little girls, so the dirty old copper, he'll be condemned to death and guillotined and I'll go and get his head out of the bran-basket and I'll spit on his filthy mug, so there.'

Gabriel shut his eyes and shivered as these atrocities were evoked. He turned to the chap:

'You hear that?' says he. 'Doesn't it make you think twice? Kids can be terrible, you know.'

'Unkoo Gabriel,' cried Zazie, 'I swear to God they're mine, the blewgenes. You've got to stand up for me, Uncle Gabriel. You've got to stand up for me. What would my momma say if she heard that you let me be insulted by a nincompoop, a noodlewit, and maybe even a Sunday driver?

'Hell,' she added, for her own benefit, in her little inner voice, 'I'm just as good as Michèle Morgan in *Camille*.' Genuinely touched by the pathos of this invocation, Gabriel displayed his indecision in these measured terms which he pronounced medza vohchay and so to speak quasi in petto:

'All the same it's a bit awkward; once a copper's got his back up . . .'

The chap sniggers.

'You certainly have got a twisted mind,' says Gabriel, blushing.

'No but really, you don't seem to realize what's hanging over your head,' says the chap, getting more and more bloodily mephistophelian: 'white-slavery, poncing, hormosessuality, eonism, balanoid hypospadias, that little lot'll earn you some ten years' hard.'

Then he turns his attention to Marceline.

'And what about Madame? A little information about Madame is likewise indicated.'

'What information?' asks Marceline gently.

'Don't say a word till your lawyer gets here,' says Zazie. 'Uncle wouldn't listen to me and now he's really in the mud.'

'Will you shut your mouth,' says the chap to Zazie. 'Yes,' he goes on, 'and could Madame tell us what profession she follows?'

'Housewife,' Gabriel replies ferociously.

'And what does that consist of?' asks the chap ironically.

Gabriel turns to Zazie and winks, so that the child shall be prepared to relish the forthcoming events to the full.

'And what does that consist of?' says he anaphorically. 'For instance in throwing out the garbage.'

He seizes the chap by the coat collar, drags him out on to the landing and projects him towards the nether regions.

This makes a noise: a muffled noise.

The titfer goes the same way. It makes less noise, even though it is a bowler.

'Terrific,' exclaimed Zazie enthusiastically, while down below the chap was picking himself up and replacing his moustache and dark glasses.

'What can I get you?' Turandot asked him.

'A pick-me-up,' replied the chap pertinently.

'Well there's lots of different brands.'

'All the same to me.'

He went and sat down at the far end.

'Well now what should I give him,' muses Turandot. 'A Fernet-Branca?'

'It's undrinkable,' says Charles.

'You've probably never tasted it. It isn't as bad as all that and it's marvellous for the stomach. You ought to try it.'

'Give us a tiny drop then,' says Charles, to keep the peace.

Turandot pours him out a large glassful.

Charles moistens his lips, emits a little lapping noise, does it again, sips pensively, his lips working, swallows that mouthful, goes on to another.

'Well?' asks Turandot.

'It's not too foul.'

'A bit more?'

Turandot fills the glass again and puts the bottle back on the shelf. He ferrets about some more and discovers something else.

'There's arquebus water, too,' says he.

'Oh that's out of date. Nowadays what we need is atomic water.'

This evocation of world history makes them all laugh like drains.

'Well well well,' exclaims Gabriel coming full steam into the bistro, 'can't say you don't sound cheerful in this establishment. Not like in my place. Such goings-on. Give me a nice strong grenadine, not much aqua pura, I need a pick-me-up. If you knew what I've been going through.'

'You can tell us later,' says Turandot, somewhat embarrassed.

'Oh it's you, hullo,' says Gabriel to Charles. 'You're staying to lunch with us?'

'Wasn't that already fixed?'

'Just reminding you, that's all.'

'Don't have to remind me. Hadn't forgotten.'

'Well let's say that I'm confirming the invitation then.'

'Don't have to confirm it since it was all fixed.'

'Then you're staying to lunch with us,' concluded Gabriel who wanted to have the last word.

'Talk talk,' said Laverdure, 'that's all you can do.'

'Drink it up then,' said Turandot to Gabriel.

Gabriel follows this advice.

'(sigh) Such goings-on. You saw Zazie come back with a chap in tow?'

'Yess,' yespered Turandot and Mado Ptits-pieds discreetly.

'I got here after,' said Charles.

'By the way,' said Gabriel, 'did you see him go by again?'

'You know,' said Turandot, 'I didn't have time to get a good look at him so I'm not absolutely sure I'd recognize him, but he could well be the chap sitting over there at the back behind you.'

Gabriel turned round. The chap was there on a chair, patiently waiting for his pick-me-up.

'Jeezers,' said Turandot, 'that's true, beg yours, I'd forgotten you.'

'Don't mention it,' said the chap politely.

'What would you say to a Fernet-Branca?'

'If that's what you recommend.'

At this moment a greenish Gabriel lets himself slide gently to the ground.

'Make it two Fernet-Brancas,' says Charles, scooping up his pal as he goes by.

'Two Fernet-Brancas, two,' Turandot replies automatically.

Events have made him somewhat nervy and he can't manage to fill the glasses, his hand shakes, he slops brownish puddles all over the place which send forth pseudopodia which in their passage pollute the wooden (since the occupation) counter.

'Oh let me do it,' says Mado Ptits-pieds, snatching the bottle out of the hands of the agitated boss.

Turandot wipes his brow. The chap peaceably sips his pick-me-up which has at last been served. Holding Gabriel's nose, Charles pours the liquid between his teeth. It dribbles out of the corners of his mouth a bit. Gabriel shakes himself.

'You dope, you,' says Charles affectionately.

'No guts,' remarks the chap, reinvigorated.

'Shouldn't say that,' says Turandot. 'He's shown his mettle. During the war.'

'What'd he do?' asks the other nonchalantly.

'STO,' replies the innkeeper, pouring out new doses of Fernet all round.

'Ah!' says the chap, quite indifferent.

'Praps you don't remember,' said Turandot. 'All the same, tsamazing how quickly people forget. Forced labour. In Germany. Don't you remember?'

'That don't necessarily prove he's tough, though,' remarks the chap.

'And the bombs,' says Turandot. 'Have you forgotten them? The bombs?'

'And what did he do with the bombs, your tough guy? Catch 'em in his arms so they didn't go off?'

'That's not very funny,' says Charles. This is beginning to get on his nerves.

'Don't argue,' murmurs Gabriel who is resuming contact with the surrounding landscape.

With a step too faltering to be true he goes over and collapses at a table which turns out to be the one the chap is sitting at. Gabriel takes a little mauve cloth out of his pocket and dabs his face with it, causing the bistro to become fragrant with moonlit amber and silvery musk.

'Pooh,' says the chap. 'Your lingerie stinks.'

'You're not going to start on me all over again, are you?' asks Gabriel, adopting a pained air. 'It happens to be one of Fior's, this perfume.'

'Have to try and understand people,' Charles tells him. 'There's some coarse individuals who don't like anything refined.'

'Refined, that's a laugh,' says the chap, 'that lot's been refined in a pooh-pooh refinery, yes indeedy.'

'You don't realize how right you are,' esclaims Gabriel blithely. 'It seems there is a drop of it in the products of the best firms.'

'Even in eau-de-cologne?' asks Turandot, timidly approaching the chosen few.

'No really, you're too thick,' says Charles. 'Don't you know that Gabriel passes on any bloody silly story without even understanding it, he's only got to hear it once.'

'Have to hear them if you're going to pass them on,' retorted Gabriel. 'Have you ever been bloody clever enough to come out with a bloody silly story you've thought up all by yourself?'

'Mustn't egzaggerate,' says the chap.

'Egzaggerate what?' demands Charles.

The chap doesn't get worked up, though.

'Don't you ever tell bloody silly stories?' he asks insidiously.

'He keeps them all to himself,' says Charles to the other two. 'He's conceited.'

'None of this,' says Turandot, 'is very clear.'

'Where did we start from?' asks Gabriel.

'I was saying that you weren't capable of thinking up all by yourself all the bloody silly stories you come out with,' says Charles.

'What bloody silly stories have I come out with?'

'Can't remember. You produce so many.'

'Then in that case you shouldn't find it too difficult to give me an example.'

'Well,' said Turandot, who had got lost, 'I'll leave you to your dissertations. The place is filling up.'

The lunchtime customers were arriving, some bringing their own grub. Laverdure could be heard uttering his talk talk that's all you can do.

'Yes,' said Gabriel pensively, 'what were we talking about?'

'Nothing,' replied the chap. 'Nothing.'

Gabriel looked at him in disgust.

'Well then,' said he. 'Well then what the hell am I doing here?'

'You came to fetch me,' said Charles. 'Remember? I'm coming to lunch with you and then we're taking Zazie to the Eiffel Tower.'

'Let's go then.'

Gabriel got up and, followed by Charles, went out, ignoring the chap.

The chap called (gesture) Mado Ptits-pieds.

'While I'm about it,' he said, 'I might as well stay and have lunch.'

On the stairs Gabriel stopped to ask his chum Charles:

'Don't you think it would have been polite to ask him too?'

7

Gridoux always lunched in his shop, this avoided his missing a customer if there should happen to be one; it's true that at this time of day there never were any. Having his lunch in his shop, therefore, presented a double advantage since as no customers appeared at that time Gridoux could eat his grub in peace. This grub was as a rule a steaming plate of mincemeat and potatoes which Mado Ptits-pieds brought him after the rush hour, round about one o'clock.

'I thought it was tripe today,' said Gridoux, diving to pick up his bottle of red wine which was hidden in a corner.

Mado Ptits-pieds shrugged her shoulders. Tripe? What tripe! And Gridoux knew it.

'What about the chap?' asked Gridoux, 'what's he up to?'

'Zfinishing his grub. Znot saying a word.'

'He's not asking any questions?'

'Not one.'

'And Turandot, isn't he talking to him?'

'Doesn't dare.'

'He's not inquisitive.'

'Tisn't that he's not inquisitive, but he doesn't dare.'

'Yerss.'

Gridoux started to attack his fodder, the temperature of which had fallen to a reasonable degree.

'To follow?' asked Mado Ptits-pieds, 'what would you like? Brie? Camembert?'

'What's the brie like?'

'Not going very fast.'

'The other then.'

As Mado Ptits-pieds was going off, Gridoux asked her:

'And the chap? what'd he have?'

'Same as you. Gzactly.'

She ran the ten yards separating the shop from La Cave. She'd answer in greater detail later. Gridoux was indeed of the opinion that the information furnished was decidedly insufficient, however he seemed to be able to use it to nourish his meditation until the servant returned and presented him with a morose piece of cheese.

'Well?' asked Gridoux. 'The chap?'

'He's finishing his coffee.'

'And what's he saying?'

'Still nothing.'

'Did he have a good meal? Good appetite?'

'On the whole. He's not one of those finicky eaters.'

'What did he have to start with? Those lovely sardines or the tomato salad?'

'Same as you like I said, gzactly the same as you. He didn't have anything to start with.'

'And to drink?'

'Red.'

'Quarter of a bottle? Half a bottle?'

'Half. He drank the lot.'

'Aha!' said Gridoux, decidedly interested.

Before attacking the cheese, with a skilful effort of suction he pensively extirpated some filaments of beef that had got wedged in among his dentition in several places.

'And what about the lav?' he asked next. 'Didn't he go to the lav?'

'No.'

'Not even to have a pee?'

'No.'

'Not even to wash his mitts?'

'No.'

'How does he look now?'

'The same.'

Gridoux starts on a vast slice of bread and cheese which he has prepared methodically, pushing the rind towards the farthest extremity, thus keeping the best for last.

Mado Ptits-pieds watches him do this with an absent-minded look, not at all in a hurry now, not that she's finished serving, there are customers who must be asking for their bills, the chap perhaps for instance. She leant against the bench and, taking advantage of the fact that while Gridoux was eating he couldn't hold forth, she started on her personal problems.

'He's a steady sort of chap,' said she. 'A man with a trade. A good trade, because it is good, a taxi, isn't it?'

'(gesture)'

'Not too old. Not too young. Healthy. Tough. Sure to have some savings. He's got everything on his side, Charles. Zonly one thing: he's too romantic.'

'Mm,' agreed Gridoux between two deglutitions.

'I can't tell you how it irritates me when I see him lapping up the lonely hearts column or the are you genuinely seeking marriage only ads in one of those women's mags. How can you possibly imagine, I say to him, how can you possibly imagine that that's where you'll find your dream girl, your bird of paradise? If she was as gorgeous as all that, your birdie, she'd find a way to fall straight out of her nest into your arms, don't you think?'

'(gesture)'

Gridoux has arrived at his last deglutition. He's finished his slice of bread, he knocks back a glass of wine in a leisurely fashion and puts away the bottle.

'What about Charles,' he asks, 'what does he say to all that?'

'He says damned silly things like: and what about your bird of paradise, does it often drop into your lap? Any old drivel, you see (sigh). Doesn't want to understand me.'

'Have to pop the question to him.'

'I've often thought of it, but I never seem to get a chance. For instance I sometimes meet him on the stairs. Then we have a bit, upstairs and downstairs, as you might say. Only then I can't talk to him like I should, I just can't concentrate on it (silence) — on talking to him like I should (silence). I have to ask him to dinner one evening. You think he'd come?'

'Any case, it wouldn't be very nice of him if he didn't.'

'Well that's just it, he isn't always very nice, Charles.'

Gridoux made a gesture signifying disagreement. On his doorstep the boss was calling: 'Mado!'

'Coming!' she replied, just loudly enough to enable her words to cleave the air with the desired speed and intensity. 'In any case,' she added, now speaking to Gridoux, and in a more subdued tone, 'what I ask myself is, what does he think she'd have that I haven't got, the floosy he'd get himself through the newspaper: a golden baba or what?'

Another owl-call from Turandot prevents her expressing other hypotheses. She takes back the crocks and Gridoux finds himself all alone with his trotter-cases and the street. He doesn't start work again straight away. He slowly rolls one of his five daily cigarettes and starts smoking it leisurely. You might almost say that it would seem as if he looks as if he's thinking about something. When the cigarette is almost finished he stubs out the butt and puts it away carefully in a throat-lozenge box, a habit dating from the occupation. Then someone asks him you haven't a shoe-lace by any chance have you I've just bust mine. Gridoux raises his eyes and he'd have been willing to bet on it, it's the chap and he goes on like this:

'Znothing more irritating, don't you think?'

'I don't know,' Gridoux answers.

'Yellow ones I need. Brown if you like, but not black.'

'I'll see what I've got,' said Gridoux. 'Can't guarantee that I've got 'em in all the colours you mention.'

He doesn't move, and merely looks at his interlocutor. Said interlocutor makes out he doesn't notice.

'After all I'm not asking for iridescent ones.'

'Which ones?'

'Rainbow-coloured ones.'

'It just so happens that I'm out of those for the moment. And the other coloured ones, I haven't got any either.'

'And over there in that box, aren't they shoe-laces?'

Gridouxgrumbles:

'Look here, you, I don't like people nosing about in my place like that.'

'All the same you surely wouldn't refuse to sell a shoe-lace to someone who has need of one. Might as well refuse a bit of bread to a starving man.'

'Oh come off it, d'you want me to burst into tears?'

'And a pair of shoes? Would you refuse to sell a pair of shoes?'

'Now there,' exclaims Gridoux, 'there you're talking through your hat.'

'And why's that?'

'I mend shoes, I don't sell 'em. Ne sutor ultra crepidam, as the ancients have it. You understand Latin, perhaps? Usque non ascendam anch'io son pittore adios amigos amen and such like. But it's true, you wouldn't be able to appreciate it, you're not a curé you're a cop.'

'Where'd you get that from, if you please?'

'A cop or a sex-maniac.'

The chap calmly shrugged his shoulders and said with neither conviction nor bitterness:

'Insults, that's all the thanks you get when you restore a lost child to her family. Insults.'

And he added after a heavy sigh:

'And what a family.'

Gridoux unstuck his buttocks from his chair and asked threateningly:

'And what's wrong with them, her family? What've you got against them?'

'Oh! nothing (smile).'

'Come on, out with it, out with it.'

'The uncle is an auntie. An Aunt Nancy.'

'Tisn't true,' yelled Gridoux, 'tisn't true, I won't let you say it.'

'There's no call for you to let me say anything, my dear fellow, I don't take orders from you.'

'Gabriel,' stated Gridoux solemnly, 'Gabriel is a respectable citizen, a respectable and honourable citizen. What's more everyone round these parts likes him.'

'He's a seductress.'

'You really make me vomit, you do indeed, you and your superior airs. I tell you, Gabriel is not a queer, have you got that, yes or no?'

'Prove it,' said the other.

'Not difficult,' replied Gridoux. 'He's married.'

'Doesn't prove a thing,' said the other. 'Take Henry the Third, for instance, he was married.'

'And who to? (smile).'

'Louise de Vaudémont.'

Gridoux cackles.

'We'd have known about it if that good lady had been Queen of France.'

'We do know about it.'

'You heard it on the telly (grimace). Maybe you believe everything they come out with?'

'Doesn't stop it being in all the books.'

'Even in the Telephone Directory?'

The chap didn't know what to say to that.

'You see,' concluded Gridoux good-naturedly.

He added these wingèd words:

'Believe me, you mustn't judge people too quickly. Gabriel dances in a queers' night club dressed up as a Spanish gipsy girl, granted. But what does that prove, eh? What does that prove. Here, give me your shoe, I'll put a lace in for you.'

The chap took his shoe off and hopped about on one foot while he waited for the exchange operation to be concluded.

'That doesn't prove a thing,' Gridoux went on, 'except that it amuses the rubes. A colossus dressed up as a toreador is funny enough, but a colossus dressed up as a gipsy girl, that's what really makes people split their sides. And anyway, that's not the whole story, he dances *The Dying Swan*, too, like they do at the Opera. In a tutu. And there people just double up laughing. You're going to talk about human folly, I agree, but it's a job like any other after all, isn't it?'

'What a job,' was all the chap said.

'What a job, what a job,' retorted Gridoux, copycatting him. 'And what about you, what about your job; are you proud of it?'

The chap didn't answer.

(double silence).

'Here,' Gridoux went on, 'here's your shoe, with its nice new lace.'

'What do I owe you?'

'Nothing,' said Gridoux.

He added:

'All the same, you aren't very chatty.'

'That's not fair, *I*'m the one who came to see you.'

'Yes, but you don't answer the questions you get asked.'

'Such as?'

'Do you like spinach?'

'With croûtons I can tolerate it, but I wouldn't do anything rash for it.'

Gridoux was pensive for a moment, then he let out a volley of jeeheezerses, uttered in a low voice.

'What's the matter?' asked the chap.

'I'd give a lot to know what brought you to these parts.'

'I came to restore a lost child to her family.'

'You'll end up by getting me to believe it.'

'And it's caused me a lot of trouble.'

'Oh,' said Gridoux, 'nothing so very terrible.'

'I'm not talking about the business with the king of the Seguidilla and the princess of the blewgenes (silence). There's something worse.'

The chap had finished putting his shoe back on.

'There's something worse,' he repeated.

'What?' asked Gridoux, upset.

'I returned the little girl to her family, but now *I*'m lost.'

'Oh! that's nothing,' said Gridoux, his equanimity restored. 'You go down the street on the left and you'll find the metro a bit further on, it's not difficult as you can see.'

'Znot a question of that. It's myself, myself, that I've lost.'

'Don't understand,' said Gridoux, once again a bit worried.

'Ask me some questions, ask me some questions, then you'll understand.'

'But you don't answer questions.'

'That's not fair! as if I didn't answer about the spinach.'

Gridoux scratched his skull.

'Well for instance . . .'

But he couldn't continue, he was highly embarrassed.

'Say it,' insisted the chap, 'go on, say it.'

(silence). Gridoux lowers his eyes.

The chap comes to his aid.

'Perhaps you'd like to know my name, for egzample?'

'Yes,' said Gridoux, 'that's it, your name.'

'Well I don't know it.'

Gridoux raised his eyes.

'Clever, eh,' said he.

'No, really, I don't know it.'

'How's that?'

'How's that? Just like that. I haven't learnt it by heart.'

(silence).

'You take me for a bloody ape,' said Gridoux.

'And why's that?'

'Do people need to learn their names by heart?'

'Well, you,' said the chap, 'what's your name?'

'Gridoux,' replied Gridoux unsuspiciously.

'So you see you *do* know it by heart, your name, Gridoux.'

'So I do,' murmured Gridoux.

'But the worst thing in my case,' went on the chap 'is that I don't even know if I had one before.'

'A name?'

'A name.'

'It's not possible,' murmured Gridoux, overwhelmed.

'Possible, possible, what d'you mean, "possible", when it *is* so?'

'Then you sort of never did have a name?'

'Seems so.'

'And hasn't that ever caused you any trouble?'

'Not too much.'

(silence).

The chap repeated:

'Not too much.'

'And your age,' Gridoux asked abruptly. 'Maybe you don't know your age either?'

'No,' replied the chap. 'Of course I don't.'

Gridoux carefully examined the aspect of his interlocutor.

'You must be about . . .'

But he interrupted himself.

'It's difficult to say,' he murmured.

'Yes, isn't it? So when you keep asking me about my job you can see that it isn't out of bloody-mindedness that I don't answer.'

'Of course,' Gridoux acquiesced, in anguish.

The sound of a ramshackle motor made the chap turn round. An old taxi went by, with Gabriel and Zazie on board.

'Going for a ride,' said the chap.

Gridoux doesn't comment. He'd be more than willing for someone to take this chap for a ride, too.

'It only remains for me to thank you,' went on the chap.

'Don't mention it,' said Gridoux.

'And the metro? Then I'll find it over there? (gesture).'

'That's right. Over there.'

'That's a useful piece of information,' said the chap. 'Particularly when there's a strike on.'

'You can always look at the map,' said Gridoux.

He started to hammer very hard on a sole and the chap departed.

8

'Ah, Paris,' cried Gabriel with greedy enthusiasm. 'Hey, Zazie,' he added abruptly, pointing at something a long way away, 'look!! the metro!!!'

'The metro?' said she.

She frowned.

'The elevated, of course,' said Gabriel blissfully.

Before Zazie had had time to bellyache he iksclaimed again:

'And that! over there!! look!!! The Panthéon!!!!'

'Tisn't the Panthéon,' said Charles, 'it's the Invalides.'

'You're not going to start all over again,' said Zazie.

'Oh go on,' cried Gabriel, 'so that isn't the Panthéon?'

'No, it's the Invalides,' replied Charles.

Gabriel turned in his direction and looked him in the cornea of the eyes:

'Are you sure about that,' he asks him, 'are you really so sure as all that?'

Charles didn't answer.

'What is there that you're absolutely sure about?' Gabriel insisted.

'I've got it,' Charles then roars, 'that thing there, tisn't the Invalides it's the Sacré-Coeur.'

'And you I suppose,' says Gabriel jovially, 'wouldn't by any chance be the sacred cow?'

'Little humorists your age,' says Zazie, 'give me the willies.'

After which they observed the orama in silence, then Zazie investigated what was going on some 300 metres below as the plumb line falls.

'Tisn't as high as all that,' Zazie remarked.

'All the same,' said Charles, 'you can only just make out the people.'

'Yes,' said Gabriel, sniffing, 'you can hardly see them but you can smell them just the same.'

'Less than in the metro,' said Charles.

'You never go in it,' said Gabriel. 'Nor do I, for that matter.'

Wishing to avoid this painful subject, Zazie said to her uncle:

'You aren't looking. Lean over, it's funny, you know.'

Gabriel made an attempt to cast an eye into the depths.

'Hell,' said he, retreating, 'it makes me giddy.'

He mopped his brow and gave off an aroma.

'Personally,' he adds, 'I'm going down. If you haven't had enough I'll wait for you on the ground floor.'

He's gone before Zazie and Charles can stop him.

'It must be twenty years since I came up it,' says Charles. 'I've driven enough people here though.'

It's all the same to Zazie.

'You don't laugh much,' says she to him. 'How old are you?'

'How old would you say I was?'

'Hm, yaren't young: thirty.'

'And fifteen on top.'

'Hm well then you don't look too old. An unkoo Gabriel?'

'Thirty-two.'

'Hm, well him now he looks older.'

'Goodness sake don't tell him so, it'd make him cry.'

'Why on earth? Because he practises hormosessuality?'

'Where did you dig that one up?'

'It was the chap who said that to uncle Gabriel, the chap who brought me back. That's what he said, the chap, that you could go to jug for that, for hormosessuality. What is it?'

'Tsnot true.'

'*Tis* true that he said that,' retorted Zazie, indignant that anyone should doubt a single one of her words.

'That's not what I mean, I mean that, about Gabriel, tisn't true what the chap said.'

'That he's a hormosessual? But what does it mean? That he uses perfume?'

'That's it. Now you know.'

'Znothing in that to go to prison for.'

'Of course there isn't.'

They mused for a moment in silence as they observed the Sacré-Coeur.

'What about you?' asked Zazie. 'Are you one, a hormosessual?'

'Do I look queer?'

'No, you look pretty ordinary to me.'

'Well then you see.'

'I don't see a thing.'

'Well I'm certainly not going to do you a drawing.'

'Are you good at drawing?'

Charles turned in the other direction and became absorbed in the contemplation of the spires of Sainte-Clotilde, the work of Gau and Ballu, and then suggested:

'Shall we go down?'

'Tell me,' asked Zazie without budging, 'why aren't you married?'

'That's life.'

'Why don't you get married?'

'Haven't found anyone who suits me.'

Zazie whistled admiringly.

'You certainly think a lot of yourself.'

'That's the way it is. But tell me, when you're grown-up, do you think there'll be so many men you'd want to marry?'

'Staminute,' said Zazie, 'what're we talking about? Men or women?'

'Sa question of women for me, and men for you.'

'There's no comparison,' said Zazie.

'Can't say you're wrong.'

'You really are funny,' said Zazie. 'You never really know what you think. It must be exhausting. Is that why you always look so solemn?'

Charles deigns to smile.

'What about me?' says Zazie, 'would I suit you?'

'You're only a brat.'

'There's some girls who get married at fifteen, at fourteen even. There's some men who like that.'

'Well then? tabout me? would I suit you?'

'Of course not,' replied Zazie with simplicity.

Having swallowed this primary truth, Charles resumed the conversation in these terms:

'You've got some funny ideas, you know, for your age.'

'Yes that's true, I even wonder myself where I get them from.'

'Well I certainly couldn't tell you.'

'Why is it that we say some things and not others?'

'If we didn't say what we have to say, we wouldn't make ourselves understood.'

'How about you, do you always say what you have to say to make yourself understood?'

'(gesture)'

'All the same nobody forces us to say anything we do say, we could say something else.'

'(gesture)'

'Well you might answer me!'

'You make me tired. All that's not questions.'

'Of course it's questions. Only it's questions you don't know how to answer.'

'I don't think I'm ready to get married just yet,' said Charles pensively.

'Oh! you know,' said Zazie 'all women don't ask questions like I do.'

'All women, just listen to her, all women. But you're only a little chick.'

'Oh! excuse me, I've already started . . .'

'That's enough. No indecencies.'

'There's nothing indecent about that. That's life.'

'It's a fine thing, life.'

He pulled at his moustache, again squinting morosely at the Sacré-Coeur.

'Life,' said Zazie, 'you ought to know all about it. They say you see some funny things in your trade.'

'Where'd you get that one from?'

'I read it in the Sunday Sanctimontronian, a rag that's pretty up to date even for the provinces, where they write about famous love-affairs, astrology and everything, well, it said there that taxi-drivers, they see it in all its aspects and of all sorts, sessuality. Starting with the customers who want to pay in kind. Zthat often happened to you?'

'Oh that'll do that'll do.'

'That's all you can say: "that'll do that'll do". You must be repressed.'

'God she makes you sick.'

'Oh come on, don't bellyache, it'd be better if you told me about your complexes.'

'Oh Jesus what next.'

'Women frighten you, eh?'

'I'm going down. Because I feel giddy. Not because of that (gesture). But because of a junior doll like you.'

He withdraws and some time later there he is again only a few feet above sea-level. Gabriel, with a dull look in his eye, was waiting, his knees wide apart and his hands resting on them. Seeing Charles without his niece he leaps up, and his face takes on an anxious-green colour.

'Oh even so you haven't done that,' exclaims he.

'You'd have heard her fall,' replies Charles as he sits down, worn out.

'Oh that wouldn't have mattered. But to leave her alone.'

'You can collect her at the exit. She won't fly away.'

'Yes but from now till she gets there, how much more trouble is she going to cause me (sigh). If only I'd known.'

Charles doesn't react.

So Gabriel looks at the tower attentively, lengthily, then comments:

'I wonder why people think of the city of Paris as a woman. With a thing like that. Before they put it up, perhaps. But now. It's like women who turn into men because they're so keen on sport. You read about it in the papers.'

'(silence)'

'Ah well, now you've lost your tongue. What do *you* think about it?'

Charles then utters a long, mournful neighing sound, clutches his head in his two hands and groans.

'Him too,' he says, still groaning, 'him too . . . always the same thing . . . always sessuality . . . always a question of that . . . always . . . all the time . . . putrefaction . . . nauseation . . . they think of nothing else . . .'

Gabriel pats him on the shoulder benevolently.

'You look as if there's something the matter,' he says casually. 'What happened?'

'It's your niece . . . your whore of a niece.'

'Oy oy, careful,' cries Gabriel, removing his hand in order to lift it up towards the heavens, 'my niece is my niece. Moderate your language, or you'll hear plenty about your grandmother.'

Charles makes a despairing gesture, then gets up abruptly.

'Ah well,' says he, 'I'm off. I'd rather not see that brat again. Farewell.'

And he goes off towards his jalopy.

Gabriel runs after him:

'How'll we get back?'

'You can take the metro.'

'Marvellous jokes he thinks up,' Gabriel grunted, giving up his pursuit.

The taks departs.

Left standing, Gabriel meditated, and then pronounced these words:

'Being or nothingness, that is the question. Ascending, descending, coming, going, a man does so much that in the end he disappears. A taxi bears him off, a metro carries him away, the Tower doesn't care, nor the Panthéon. Paris is but a dream, Gabriel is but a reverie (a charming one), Zazie the dream of a reverie (or of a nightmare) and all this story the dream of a dream, the reverie of a reverie, scarcely more than the typewritten delirium of an idiotic novelist (oh! sorry). Over there, farther – a little farther – than the Place de la République, the graves are overflowing with Parisians who were, who ascended and descended the stairs, came and went in the streets, and who did so much that in the end they disappeared. Forceps bore them, a hearse carries them away, and the Tower rusts and the Panthéon cracks more rapidly than the bones of the dead who are too much with us dissolve in the humus of the town impregnated with cares. But *I* am alive, and there ends my knowledge, for of the taximann, fled in his locatory jalopy, or of my niece, suspended a thousand feet up in the atmosphere, or of my spouse the gentle Marceline, left guarding the household gods, I know nothing at this precise moment, here and now, I know nothing but this, alexandrinarily: that they are almost dead because they are not here. But what do I see above the hairy noddles of the good people who surround me?'

Some travellers were standing in a circle round him, having taken him for a supplementary guide. They turned their heads to see what he was looking at.

'And what *do* you see?' asked one of them, particularly versed in the French language.

'Yes,' approved another. 'What is there to see?'

'Indeed,' adds a third, 'what ought we to see?'

'Tweetosee?' asked a fourth, 'tweetosee? tweetosee? tweetosee?'

'Tiutosee?' replied Gabriel, 'why (grand gesture) Zazie, my niece Zazie, who is issuing forth from the ironmongery and wending her way towards us.'

Cameras crepitate, then the travellers make way for the child. Who cackles.

'Well, uncle? doing a good trade?'

'As you see,' replied Gabriel with satisfaction.

Zazie shrugged her shoulders and looked at the audience. She didn't see Charles in their midst and drew attention to that fact.

'He beat it,' said Gabriel.

'Why?'

'No reason.'

'No reason, that's not an answer.'

'Oh wurl, he just went.'

'He must have had a reason.'

'Oh you know, Charles (gesture).'

'You don't want to tell me?'

'You know why as well as I do.'

A traveller intervened:

'Male bonas horas collocamus si non dicis isti puellae weshalb dieser Mann Karl weggegangen ist.'

'My dear little fellow,' replied Gabriel, 'mind your own Geschäft. Sie weiss warum und sie ärgert mich sehr.'

'Oy oy,' exclaimed Zazie. 'Now it seems you can talk ouslandish languages.'

'I didn't do it on purpose,' replied Gabriel modestly, lowering his eyes.

'Höchst interessant,' said one of the travellers.

Zazie returned to her point of departure.

'All this doesn't tell me why Charlesbuggadorff.'

Gabriel got annoyed.

'Because you were talking about things he didn't understand. Things not suitable for someone his age.'

'Well, unkoo Gabriel, supposing I said things to you that you didn't understand, things not suitable for someone your age, what'd you do?'

'Try,' said Gabriel in an apprehensive voice.

'For egzample,' went on Zazie relentlessly, 'if I asked you, are you a hormosessual or aren't you? would you understand? Dthat be suitable for someone your age?'

'Höchst interessant.' said a traveller (same one as before).

'Poor Charles,' sighed Gabriel.

'Are you going to answer, yes or nosepick,' shouted Zazie. 'Do you understand the word: hormosessual?'

'Of course,' yelled Gabriel, 'want me to do you a drawing?'

The crowd, interested, expressed approval. A few applauded.

'Ywouldn't have the guts to,' retorted Zazie.

It was then that Fyodor Balanovitch appeared on the scene.

'Come on, get a move on!' he started to holler. 'Schnell! Schnell! back into the coach, and at the double.'

'Dove andiamo adesso?'

'To the Sainte-Chapelle,' replied Fyodor Balanovitch. 'That gem of Gothic art. Come on, get a move on. Schnell! Schnell!'

But the people didn't get a move on, greatly interested as they were by Gabriel and his niece.

'There,' the latter was saying to the former, who hadn't drawn anything, 'you see you didn't have the guts to.'

'God what a bore she can be,' the former was saying.

Fyodor Balanovitch, having confidently climbed aboard his lugger, perceived that he had only been followed by three or four mental defectives.

'Oy, you lot,' he bawled, 'what's happened to your discipline? What're they bloody well doing, my God!'

He hooted a few times. Which caused no one to budge. But a cop gave him a dirty look. As Fyodor Balanovitch had no desire to engage in vocal conflict with an individual of that species, he climbed down from his driving seat again and directed his steps towards the group formed by his administrees in order to discover what could be luring them into insubordination.

'But it's Gabriella,' he exclaimed. 'What the devil are you doing here?'

'Sh sh,' said Gabriel, while the circle of his admirers went into naïve raptures at the sight of this encounter.

'No really though,' went on Fyodor Balanovitch, 'you're surely not going to treat them to *The Dying Swan* in a tutu, are you?'

'Shh shh,' said Gabriel again, very short of conversation.

'And what's this brat you're carting around with you? Where d'you pick her up?'

'That's my niece and kindly try and show some respect for my family, minor though it be.'

'And that chap, who's he?' asked Zazie.

'A pal,' said Gabriel. 'Fyodor Balanovitch.'

'You see,' said Fyodor Balanovitch to Gabriel, 'I'm not doing Paris *bâille-naïte* any more, I've gone up in the social hierarchy and I'm taking all these clot-faces to the Sainte-Chapelle.'

'Maybe you could take us home. With this strike of the public transpiration you can't do anything you want to any more. Not a taks to be seen.'

'We're not going home yet,' said Zazie.

'In any case,' said Fyodor Balanovitch, 'we'll have to go to the Sainte-Chapelle first before it closes. After that,' he added, to Gabriel, 'I might possibly take you home.'

'And is it interesting, the Sainte-Chapelle?' asked Gabriel.

'Sainte-Chapelle! Sainte-Chapelle!' such was the touristic clamour and those who uttered it, this touristic clamour, swept Gabriel along with them to the coach with irresistible impetus.

'They've fallen for him,' said Fyodor Balanovitch to Zazie, who, like him, was left behind.

'All the same you needn't,' said Zazie 'think I'm going to let myself be carted round with all those sheep.'

'I,' said Fyodor Balanovitch, 'don't give a bugger.'

And he climbed up again behind the steering wheel and his mike, immediately utilizing this last-mentioned instrument:

'Come on, get a move on,' he loud-spoke jovially. 'Schnell! Schnell!'

Gabriel's admirers had already installed him comfortably and, equipped with adequate apparatuses, were measuring the weight of the light in order to take his portrait with a silhouette effect. Albeit all these attentions flattered him, he enquired nevertheless as to the fate of his niece. Having learnt from Fyodor Balanovitch that said niece refused to follow the crowd, he snatched himself out of the magic circle of xenophonics, got out again and threw himself on Zazie whom he seized by one arm and dragged along to the coach.

The cameras crepitated.

'You're hurting me,' yelped Zazie, mad with rage.

But she too was carried along towards the Sainte-Chapelle by the vehicle with the heavy pneumatic tyres.

9

'Open wide your peepers, clots and clotesses,' said Fyodor Balanovitch.
'On your right you are about to see the Gare d'Orsay. It's very in-te-res-
ting, architecturally, and it'll make up for the Sainte-Chapelle, if we
arrive too late which is what's staring you in the face with all these
bleeding traffic holdups on account of this stinking strike.'

Communing in unanimous and total incomprehension, the travellers gaped. The most fanatic amongst them hadn't in any case paid
the slightest attention to the snarls of the loudspeaker and, perched
the wrong way round on top of their seats, they were contemplating
with emotion the archguide Gabriel. He smiled at them. Therefore
they hoped.

'Sainte-Chapelle,' they tried to say. 'Sainte-Chapelle.'

'Yes yes,' he said amiably. 'The Sainte-Chapelle (silence) (gesture)
that gem of Gothic art (gesture) (silence).'

'Don't start talking crap all over again,' said Zazie sourly.

'Go on, go on,' cried the travellers, drowning the child's voice.
'We want to hearken, we want to hearken,' they added in a great
berlitzscoulian effort.

'All the same you're not going to let them make a fool of you
like that,' said Zazie.

Through the material of his trousers she seized a piece of his flesh
between her nails and twisted it viciously. The pain was so intense
that great big tears began to flow down Gabriel's cheeks. The
travellers who, in spite of their wide experience of cosmopolitanism,
had never yet seen a guide cry, were worried; analysing this strange
behaviour, some according to deductive reasoning, others according
to inductive, they came to the conclusion that an unguentum aureum

77

was called for. A collection was made and placed on the knees of the poor man whose face became all smiles again, more it must be added because of the cessation of his sufferings than out of gratitude, because the sum was not considerable.

'All this must seem very odd to you,' he said to the travellers bashfully.

A rather distinguished francophonic lady expressed the general opinion.

'What about the Sainte-Chapelle?'

'Aha,' said Gabriel and he made a grand gesture.

'He is about to speak,' said the polyglot lady to her congeners in their native idiom.

Some of them, encouraged, climbed up on to the seats in order not to miss anything of the speech and the mime. Gabriel cleared his throat to give himself confidence. But Zazie did it again.

'Owch,' said Gabriel distinctly.

'Poor man,' exclaimed the lady.

'Little cow,' muttered Gabriel, rubbing his thigh.

'I,' Zazie breathed into his earflap, ''m going to beat it next time the lights are red. So you know what to do, unkoo.'

'Then after, how'll we get home?' said Gabriel groaning.

'I tell you I don't want to go home.'

'But they'll follow us . . .'

'If we don't get out,' said Zazie ferociously, 'I'll tell them you're a hormosessual.'

'In the first place,' said Gabriel calmly, 'it's not true, and, secondimo, they wouldn't understand.'

'Well, if it's not true, why did the sex-maniac call you that?'

'Ah excuse me, (gesture). It has by no means been established that he *was* a sex-maniac.'

'Hell what more do you want, then.'

'What more do I want? Facts!'

And once again he made a grand gesture with an air of illumination which greatly impressed the travellers, already fascinated by the mystery of this conversation which to its difficulty of vocabulary united so many exotic associations of ideas.

'Anyway,' added Gabriel, 'when you brought him along you told us he was a cop.'

'Yes, but now I say he was a sex-maniac. Anyhow you don't know anything about them.'

'Oh excuse me (gesture), but I do, you know.'

'You *do* know?'

'Certainly,' replied Gabriel, provoked, 'I've often had occasion to repel the advances of such people. That surprise you?'

Zazie burst out laughing.

'It doesn't surprise *me* in the least,' said the francophonic lady who understood vaguely that the subject under discussion was complexes. 'Oh! but!! not in the least!!!'

And she eyed the colossus with a certain langour.

Gabriel blushed and straightened his tie, having verified with a nimble and discreet finger that his flies were properly done up.

'Well well,' said Zazie, who'd had enough of laughing, 'you're a real family uncle. What do you say, do we scram?'

She pinched him severely again. Gabriel jumped, yelling owch. Naturally he could have clocked her one good and proper so's to deprive her of two teeth or three, her, the young chick, that is, but what'd his admirers have said? He preferred to disappear from the field of their vision rather than leave them with the pustulous and reprehensible image of the wicked Uncle. An appreciable traffic-jam happening to present itself, Gabriel, followed by Zazie, calmly got out of the coach, making little conspiratorial signs to the disconcerted travellers as they did so, a hypocritical manoeuvre which was intended to fool them. As it turned out, the said travellers were carried away before they had a chance to take any adequate action. As for Fyodor Balanovitch, the comings and goings of Gabriella left him completely cold, and all he was bothering about was leading his lambs to the required locality before the hour when museum attendants go for their libations, such a lacuna in their programme not being rectifiable for the next day the travellers were leaving for Gibraltar, city of ancient parapets. Such was their itinerary.

Zazie watched them disappear, gave a little laugh, and then, by force of a rapidly acquired habit, she seized through the material of his trousers a bit of the flesh of the thigh of her uncle between her nails and set it in helicoidal motion.

'Oh look here bloody hell,' yelled Gabriel, 'it's not funny eh bloody hell that little game, haven't you got that yet?'

'Unkoo Gabriel,' said Zazie calmly, 'you haven't esplained yet if you're a hormosessual or not, primo, and secondimo where you fished up all those beautiful things in ouslandish languages that you were spouting earlier on? Answer me.'

'Not so easy to put off, for a little chick, are you,' observed Gabriel languidly.

'Answer me, will you,' and she gave him a good kick on the ankle.

Gabriel started hopping about on one foot making faces.

'Ow-oo,' said he 'owch oy oy ooch.'

'Answer me,' said Zazie.

A bourgeoise who was cruising around in the neighbourhood went up to the child in order to say these words to her:

'Oh come now, darling, you're hurting the poor meussieu. You mustn't bully grown-ups like that.'

'Grown-ups my arse,' retorted Zazie. 'He won't answer my questions.'

'That's no excuse. Violence, my darling, must always be avoided in human relationships. It is eminently to be condemned.'

'Condemned my arse,' retorted Zazie, 'and anyway we've had enough of you, go home, it's your bedtime.'

'No, it's only four-fifteen,' said the bourgeoise.

'Can't you leave the child alone,' said Gabriel who had sat down on a bench.

'And you seem to be a peculiar sort of educator, I might add,' said the lady.

'Educator my arse,' such was Zazie's comment.

'It's obvious, you only have to listen to her speaking (gesture), such vulgarity,' said the lady showing all the signs of lively disgust.

'Oh now really, mind your own buttocks,' said Gabriel. 'I have my own ideas about education.'

'And what are they?' asked the lady, placing hers on the bench beside Gabriel.

'First of all, primo, understanding.'

Zazie sat down on the other side of Gabriel and pinched him only a tiny little bit.

'And what about *my* question?' she asked mincingly. 'Nobody going to answer it?'

'Just the same I can't throw her in the Seine,' muttered Gabriel, rubbing his thigh.

'You must be understanding,' said the bourgeoise with her most charming smile.

Zazie leant forward and said to her:

'Have you finished making eyes at my unkoo? He's married, you know.'

'Mademoiselle, your insinuations are not such as one should subtricate about a lady in the state of widowhood.'

'If only I could beat it,' muttered Gabriel.

'You'll answer me first,' said Zazie.

Gabriel looked at the blue of the sky, putting up a show of the most total disinterest.

'He doesn't look as if he wants to,' remarked the widowed lady objectively.

'He'll have to.'

And Zazie made as if she were going to pinch him. The uncle leapt up before he'd even been touched. The two persons of the feminine sex rejoiced greatly at this. The older, moderating the convulsive movements of her laughter, formulated the following question:

'And what is it you want him to tell you?'

'If he's hormosessual or not.'

'Him?' asked the bourgeoise (a pause). 'Zno doubt about it.'

'No doubt: about what?' demanded Gabriel in a fairly threatening tone.

'That you are one.'

This seemed to her to be so very funny that she chortled.

'No but look here,' said Gabriel, giving her a little pat on the back which made her drop her handbag.

'It's quite impossible to talk to you,' said the widow, picking up various objects scattered about on the asphalt.

'You're not very nice to the lady,' said Zazie.

'And it isn't by avoiding answering a child's questions that one educates it,' added the widow, sitting down beside him once again.

'You must be more understanding,' added Zazie hypocritically.

Gabriel ground his teeth.

'Come on, out with it, are you one or aren't you?'

'No no and no,' replied Gabriel firmly.

'They all say that,' remarked the lady, not convinced at all.

'Really though,' said Zazie, 'I would like to know whatitiz.'

'What?'

'What a hormosessual is.'

'Because you don't know?'

'I can guess all right but I'd like him to tell me.'

'And what do you guess?'

'Unkoo, just take out your hanky a moment.'

Gabriel, sighing, obeyed. The whole street became fragrant.

'Got it?' Zazie subtly asked the widow, who remarks in an undertone:

'Fior's Barbouze.'

'Just so,' said Gabriel, putting his handkerchief back in his pocket. 'A man's perfume.'

'Mm, that's true,' said the widow.

And to Zazie:

'You haven't guessed anything at all.'

Zazie, horribly annoyed, turned to Gabriel:

'Then why did the chap accuse you of being one?'

'What chap?' asked the lady.

'Well he accused *you* of walking the streets,' retorted Gabriel, getting his own back.

'What streets?' asked the lady.

'Owoooh,' cried Gabriel.

'Don't go *too* far, my child,' said the lady with false indulgence.

'Don't need your advice.'

And Zazie pinched Gabriel again.

'Kids really are charming,' murmured Gabriel absent-mindedly, assuming his martyrdom.

'If you don't like children,' said the bourgeoise, 'one wonders why you undertake their education.'

'That,' said Gabriel, 'is a long story.'

'Tell it to me.'

'No thanks,' said Zazie. 'I know it.'

'But *I*,' said the widow, 'don't know it.'

'Who cares about you. Well, unkoo, what about that answer?'

'I've already told you, no, no and no.'

'It's not so easy to put her off,' observed the lady, who imagined this judgment to be original.

'A real little mule,' said Gabriel tenderly.

The lady next made this remark, which was no less discerning than its predecessor:

'You don't seem to know her very well, this child. It almost looks as if you are only now discovering her various qualities.'

She rolled the word qualities between inverted commas.

'Qualities my arse,' muttered Zazie.

'You're fly,' said Gabriel. 'Zit so happens I've only had her on my hands since yesterday.'

'So I see.'

'What does she see?' demanded Zazie sourly.

'How should she know?' said Gabriel shrugging his shoulders.

Ignoring this somewhat pejorative parenthesis, the widow added:

'And she's your niece?'

'Gzactly,' replied Gabriel.

'And he's my uncle and he's queer,' added Zazie who thought this was a fairly new joke for which she was ikscused in view of her youth.

'Hello!' cried some people who were getting out of a taxi.

The most fanatic of the travellers, with the francophonic lady at their head, having got over their surprise, were pursuing their archguide through the lutetian labyrinth and the magma of traffic jams and had just with the devil's own luck got their hands on him again. They manifested great joy, for they were so entirely without malice that they didn't even suspect that they had any reason to bear any. Seizing hold of Gabriel with cries of Montjoie Sainte-Chapelle!

they dragged him to their vehicle, inserted him within it not without skill and piled in on top of him so that he should no more take wing before he had shown them their favourite monument in all its details. They didn't bother about taking Zazie along with them. The francophonic lady merely made her a friendly little sign of an ironic pseudoconspiratoriality as the hack drove off, while the other lady, no less francophonic it must be added but widowed, kept jumping up and down and vociferating. The citizens and citizenesses who happened to be in that part of the world at that point of time folded themselves up into positions which were less exposed to the shemozzle.

'If you carry on bawling like that,' Zazie nagged, 'a cop's quite capable of turning up.'

'Stupid little thing,' said the widow, 'that's just why I'm shouting: stop, guidenappers, stop, guidenappers.'

Finally a copper does come on the scene, alerted by the old duck's bleating.

'Summing up?' asks he.

'Nobody rang for you,' says Zazie.

'Well you're certainly making a riot and a rumpus,' say the copper.

'A man has just been abducted,' says the gasping lady. 'A good-looking man at that.'

'Jeez,' murmured the copman, his appetite whetted.

'My aunt Nancy,' said Zazie.

'And the man?' asked the copper.

'He's the one that's my aunt Nancy, dumbwit.'

'Well her then?'

He indicated the widow.

'Her? She's nothing.'

The policemann held his tongue, to assimilate the flavour of the situation. The lady, stimulated by the zazic epithet, there and then conceived an audacious project.

'Let us pursue the guidenappers,' says she, 'and at the Sainte-Chapelle we shall deliver him.'

'That's a tidy step from here,' remarked the constable matter-of-factly. 'I'm not a cross-country champion myself.'

'Well all the same you don't expect us to take a taxi that I'd have to pay for.'

'She's right,' said Zazie who was close-fisted. 'She's less of a half-wit than I thought.'

'Oh thank you,' said the lady, delighted.

'Don't mention it,' retorted Zazie.

'All the same that was nice,' insisted the lady.

'Oh all right all right,' said Zazie modestly.

'When you've finished your bowing and scraping,' said the copman.

'Nobody asked you to do anything,' said the lady.

'Isn't that women all over,' exclaimed the constable. 'What d'you mean you didn't ask me to do anything? You just merely ask me to give myself a stitch in my side, yes. If that's not anything, well then, from now on I don't understand anything about anything.'

He added with a nostalgic air:

'Words don't have the same meaning as they did.'

And he sighed as he looked at the extremity of his beetle-crushers.

'None of this gives me back my unkoo,' said Zazie. 'They'll start saying that I got a phobia again and it won't be true.'

'Don't worry, my child,' said the widow. 'I shall be there to bear witness to your good will and to your innocence.'

'When people really are, innocent, that is,' said the constable, 'they don't need anybody.'

'The bastard,' said Zazie, 'I can see him coming a mile off. They're all the same.'

'You know them as well as that, then, my poor child?'

'Don't talk to me about 'em, my poor lady,' replies Zazie, simpering. 'Just fancy, my mamma, she split open my papa's skull with a chopper. So after that, cops, talk about getting to know them, my dear.'

'Well I never,' said the constable.

'Cops though, they're just nothing,' said Zazie. 'But judges. Well now, that lot . . .'

'All swine,' said the constable impartially.

'Anyhow, the cops and the judges too,' said Zazie, 'I fooled 'em. Like that (gesture).'

The widow looked at her in amazement.

'How about me,' said the constable, 'how're you going to set about fooling me?'

Zazie examined him.

'Now you,' said she, 'I've seen your face before somewhere.'

'That would surprise me,' said the copman.

'Why should it? Why shouldn't I have seen you before somewhere?'

'Yes indeed,' said the widow. 'The little girl's right.'

'Oh thank you, madame,' said Zazie.

'Don't mention it.'

'Oh but I want to.'

'They're having me on,' muttered the constable.

'Well?' said the widow. 'Is that all you can do? Get moving, can't you?'

'Personally,' said Zazie, 'I'm sure I've seen him somewhere.'

But the widow had suddenly transferred her admiration to the copper.

'Don't hide your light under a bushel,' said she, accompanying these words with an aphrodisiac and vulcanizing leer. 'A handsome policeman like you must know a thing or two. Within the limits of the law, of course.'

'He's a wet,' said Zazie.

'No no,' said the lady. 'Must encourage him. Must be understanding.'

And once more she looked at him with a humid and thermogenic eye.

'Just you wait,' said the copman, suddenly galvanized into action, 'and you'll see what you'll see. You'll see what Trouscaillon is capable of.'

'He's called Trouscaillon,' cried Zazie, full of enthusiasm.

'Well *I*,' said the widow, blushing just the tiniest bit, ''m called Madame Mouaque. Like everybody else,' she added.

10

Because of the strike of the funiculars and metrolleybuses, an inflated quantity of miscellaneous vehicles was circulating in the streets, while all along the pavements tired or impatient pedestrians or pedestriennes were hitch-hiking, the principle of their success being based on the unwonted solidarity which the difficulties of the situation must have induced among the propertied classes.

Trouscaillon also took up his stand at the side of the road and, pulling a whistle out of his pocket, he extracted from it several excruciating sounds.

The cars that were passing continued on their way. Some cyclists uttered a few joyful cries and went on, carefree, to meet their destiny. The two-wheeled motorized vehicles increased the decibility of their uproar, and did not stop. Anyway it wasn't to them that Trouscaillon was making application.

There was a blank. A radical jam was no doubt freezing all the traffic somewhere or other. Then a saloon car, isolated but perfectly ordinary, appeared on the scene. Trouscaillon warbled. This time, the vehicle braked.

'What's the matter,' the driver aggressively demanded of Trouscaillon who was walking up to him. 'I haven't done anything wrong. I know the highway code. Never been had up. My papers are in order. So what? You'd be better employed if you went and got the metro working instead of coming and buggering up honest citizens. Not satisfied? Hell, what more d'you want, then?'

He departs.

'Bravo Trouscaillon,' cries Zazie from afar, assuming an extremely solemn air.

'Mustn't humiliate him like that,' said the widow Mouaque, 'it'll cramp his style.'

'I was right when I said he was a wet.'

'Don't you think he's a good-looking young man?'

'Not so long ago,' said Zazie severely, 'it was my uncle you fancied. Do you need 'em all?'

A flourish of high-pitched sounds drew their attention once more to the exploits of Trouscaillon. They were minimal. The traffic-jam must have uncorked itself somewhere, a trickle of vehicles was slowly flowing in front of the copman, but his little whistle didn't seem to impress anyone at all. Then once again the stream became rarefied, a coagulation having no doubt occurred at X.

A perfectly ordinary saloon car appeared on the scene. Trouscaillon warbled. The vehicle stopped.

'What's the matter?' the driver aggressively demanded of Trouscaillon who was walking up to him. 'I haven't done anything wrong. I've got my driving licence. Never been had up. My papers are in order. So what? You'd be better employed if you went and got the metro working again instead of coming and buggering up honest citizens. Not satisfied? Hell, go and get stuffed by the Moroccans then.'

'Oh!' exclaimed Trouscaillon, shocked.

But the chap's gone.

'Bravo, Trouscaillon,' cries Zazie at the height of the enthusiasm in which she is ecstatically swimming.

'I like him more and more,' said the widow Mouaque under her breath.

'She's absolutely nuts,' said Zazie likewise.

Trouscaillon, embarrassed, began to doubt the virtue of his uniform and whistle. He was engaged in shaking the said object to drain it of all the saliva he had poured into it when a perfectly ordinary saloon car of its own free will came and pulled up in front of him. A head stuck itself out of the carriage-work and pronounced the following hopeful words:

'Excuse me, officer, could you possibly tell me the quickest way to get to the Sainte-Chapelle, that gem of Gothic art?'

'Well,' replied Trouscaillon automatically, 'what you do, first you turn left, and then right, and then when you get to a square of somewhat exiguous dimensions you take the third on the right, then the second to the left, a bit to the right again, three times to the left, and finally straight on for fifty-five yards. Naturally in all that there'll be some one-way streets which won't simplify things for you much.'

'I'll never make it,' said the driver. 'And to think I came specially from Saint-Montron just for that.'

'Cheer up,' said Trouscaillon. 'Just a suggestion, suppose I come with you?'

'You must have other things to do.'

'Not at all, not at all, I'm as free as the heir. Only, if it was an effect of your benevolence also to convey these two persons (gesture).'

'Tsall the same to me. So long as I arrive before the time that it shuts at.'

'My word,' said the widow from afar, 'it looks as if he's finally requisitioned a conveyance.'

'I'll believe that when I see it,' said Zazie objectively.

Trouscaillon galloped over in their direction for a moment and said to them inelegantly:

'Come over here quick! The chap's taking us aboard.'

'Come on,' said the widow Mouaque, 'stop, guidenappers!'

'Goodness, I'd forgotten them,' said Trouscaillon.

'Probably be better not to talk about them to your chap,' said the widow diplomatically.

'You mean just like that,' demanded Zazie, 'he's taking us to the chapel in question?'

'Will you get a move on!'

Trouscaillon and the widow Mouaque each took Zazie by one arm, bore down upon the perfectly ordinary saloon car, and threw her into it.

'I don't like being treated like that,' howled Zazie mad with rage.

'You look like kidnappers,' said the Sanctimontronian waggishly.

'Only superficially,' said Trouscaillon, sitting down beside him. 'You'd better get going if you want to arrive before it shuts.'

They drove off. To help them on their way, Trouscaillon leant out of the window and whistled frantically. It did, nevertheless, have a certain effect. The provincial was delighted.

'Now you have to turn left,' Trouscaillon ordered.

Zazie was sulking.

'Well,' said the widow Mouaque hypocritically, 'aren't you pleased to be going to see your uncle again?'

'Uncle my arse,' said Zazie.

'Good lord,' said the driver, 'it's Jeanne Lalochère's daughter. I hadn't recognized her dressed up as a boy.'

'You know her?' asked the widow Mouaque with indifference.

'And how,' said the chap.

And he turned round to complete the identification, just time enough to collide with the car in front of him.

'Hell,' said Trouscaillon.

'It's her all right,' said the Sanctimontronian.

'*I* don't know *you*,' said Zazie.

'Well well, just a learner, eh?' said the collidee who had got down from his seat to exchange a few sizzling insults with his collider. 'Ah, no wonder . . . a provincial . . . Instead of coming and cluttering up the streets of Paris you'd be better off looking after yorduxnyorgeese.'

'But meussieu,' said the widow Mouaque, 'you are delaying us with your didactic remarks! We are on a special mission. We are on our way to rescue a guidenappee.'

'What, what?' said the Sanctimontronian, 'then I'm not playing any more. Didn't come to Paris to play cowboys and Indians.'

'What's the matter with you,' said the other driver to Trouscaillon, 'what're you waiting for, why don't you take some particulars?'

'Don't worry,' replied Trouscaillon, 'I've got it all particularized. Can rely on me.'

And he gave an imitation of a cop scribbling a lot of stuff in a dog-eared old notebook.

'Got your registration book?'

Trouscaillon pretended to examine it.

'Haven't got a diplomatic passport?'

'(discouraged negation).'

'That'll be all right,' says Trouscaillon, 'you can beat it.'

The collidee, in a daze, got back into his car and went on his way. Not the Sanctimontronian, though, he wasn't budging.

'Well!' said the widow Mouaque, 'what're you waiting for?'

Behind them, the hooters were becoming querulous.

'I tell you I don't want to play cowboys and Indians. Doesn't take a minute to stop a stray bullet.'

'In my home town,' said Zazie, 'they aren't such yellow-bellies.'

'Oh you,' said the chap, 'I know you. You could even get angels to fight a duel.'

'That's a bastardly thing to say,' said Zazie. 'Why are you trying to give me such a filthy reputation?'

The hooters were howling with increasing vigour, a real storm.

'Get going, for goodness sake!' yelled Trouscaillon.

'Discretion is the better part of valour,' said the Sanctimontronian, the coward.

'Don't worry,' said the widow Mouaque, always the diplomat. 'Zno danger. Just a joke.'

The chap turned round to inspect the appearance of the old duck in greater detail. This examination disposed him to confidence.

'You promise?' asked he.

'I've just told you so.'

'Tisn't some sort of political business with all sorts of bleeding awful consequences?'

'Of course not, it's just a joke, don't worry.'

'Well, let's go, then,' said the chap, even now not completely reassured.

'Since you say you know me,' said Zazie, 'you haven't seen my momma by any chance have you? She's in Paris too.'

They had barely covered a distance of a few lengths when the clock of a nearby church struck four, the church being in the neo-classical style, incidentally.

'We've had it,' said the Sanctimontronian.

He braked once more, which provoked a new explosion of sonorous signals behind him.

'Tsnot worth it,' he added. 'It'll be shut now.'

'All the more reason to hurry,' said the widow Mouaque, reasonable and strategic. 'We won't be able to find our guidenappee any more.'

'What do I care,' said the chap.

But there was such a racket from the hooting behind him that he couldn't help starting up again, propelled as it were by the vibrations of the air agitated by the unanimous irritation of the stoppees.

'Come on,' said Trouscaillon, 'don't sulk. We're nearly there now. So at any rate you'll be able to tell the people where you come from that even if you didn't manage to see it, the Sainte-Chapelle, at least you weren't very far away from it. While if you stay here . . .'

'You know he doesn't talk badly when he wants to,' remarked Zazie impartially apropos of the copman's dissertation.

'More and more do I like him,' breathed the widow Mouaque in a voice so low that no one heard her.

'And what about my momma,' asked Zazie once again, 'since you say you know me, you haven't seen her by any chance have you?'

'Well Ida know,' said the Sanctimontronian, 'I really am an unlucky bastard. All these jalopies around and it had to be mine you picked on.'

'We didn't do it on purrpuss,' said Trouscaillon. 'It happens to me too, when I'm in a town I don't know, I ask my way.'

'Yes but,' said the Sanctimontronian, 'how's about the Sainte-Chapelle?'

'That, it must be admitted,' said Trouscaillon who, in this simple ellipsis was making hyperbolical use of the vicious circle of the parabole.

'Right,' said the Sanctimontronian, 'let's go, then.'

'Stop, guidenappers,' cried the widow Mouaque.

And Trouscaillon, sticking his head out of the carriage-work, whistled to scatter the importunate. They advanced at a mediocre speed.

'This,' said Zazie, 'is lousy. Personally I only like the metro.'

'I've never set foot in it,' said the widow.

'Oo aren't you a snob,' said Zazie.

'So long as I have the means . . .'

'Doesn't alter the fact that you weren't prepared to cough up for a taxi earlier on.'

'There was no need to. As you see.'

'We're moving,' said Trouscaillon, turning round to the passengers to beg a little approval.

'Yehess,' said the widow Mouaque in ecstasy.

'You needn't pile it on,' said Zazie. 'By the time we get there my unkoo will have been gone ages.'

'I'm doing my best,' said the Sanctimontronian who, changing the subject, ksclaimed: 'Ah, if only we had the metro in Saint-Montron! What would you say to that, ducks?'

'Now that,' said Zazie, 'is the kind of crap-talking that particularly nauseates me. Zif we could have the metro in our dump.'

'It'll come one day,' said the chap. 'As we progress. There'll be the metro everywhere. It'll be super-smashing at that. The metro and the helicopter, there's the future so far as urban transport is concerned. You take the metro to go to Marseille and you come back by helicopter.'

'Why not the other way round?' asked the widow Mouaque whose nascent passion had not yet entirely obnubilated her native cartesianism.

'Why not the other way round?' said the chap anaphorically. 'Because of the speed of the wind.'

He looks round for a moment to estimate the impression this major witticism has made astern, the consequence being that forrard he runs smack into a double-parked coach. They'd arrived. Sure enough Fyodor Balanovitch appeared on the scene and started to deliver the sort of peroration that goes:

'Well well! Just a learner, eh? Ah, no wonder . . . a provincial . . . Instead of coming and cluttering up the streets of Paris you'd be better off looking after yorduxnyorgeese.'

'Hey,' cried Zazie, 'it's Fyodor Balanovitch. Haven't seen my unkoo have you?'

'Stop, uncle,' said the widow Mouaque, estracting herself from the cartilage.

'Oy oy, can't get away with it like that,' said Fyodor Balanovitch. 'Have to have a look-see, look at that, you've damaged the tool of my trade.'

'You were double-parked,' said the Sanctimontronian, 'tsnot done.'

'Don't start an argument,' said Trouscaillon, also getting out. 'I'll see to it.'

'That's not fair,' said Fydor Balanovitch, 'you were in his car. You'll be prejudiced.'

'Oh well, sort it out for yourselves,' said Trouscaillon, and he took his leave, anxious to rejoin the widow Mouaque, which lady had disappeared in the wake of little Zazie.

22

On the terrace of the Café des Deux Palais, Gabriel, knocking back his fifth grenadine, was holding forth to an assembly whose attention seemed all the greater in that its francophony was more diffuse.

'Why,' he was saying, 'why should one not tolerate this life, since so little suffices to deprive one of it? So little brings it into being, so little brightens it, so little blights it, so little bears it away. Otherwise, who would tolerate the blows of fate and the humiliations of a successful career, the swindling of grocers, the prices of butchers, the water of milkmen, the irritation of parents, the fury of teachers, the bawling of sergeant-majors, the turpitude of the beats, the lamentations of the dead-beats, the silence of infinite space, the smell of cauliflower or the passivity of the wooden horses on a merry-go-round, were it not for his knowledge that the bad and proliferative behaviour of certain minute cells (gesture) or the trajectory of a bullet traced by an involuntary, irresponsible, anonymous individual might unexpectedly come and cause all these cares to evaporate into the blue of the heavens. I, who now address you, have many times orientated my thoughts towards these problems while, dressed in a tutu, I expose to cretins like you my naturally fairly hirsute it must be admitted but professionally epilated thighs. I should add that if you so desire you can be present at this spectacle this very evening.'

'Hurrah!' cried the travellers confidently.

'Well Ida know Unkoo, trade's getting better and better.'

'Ah, there you are,' said Gabriel calmly. 'Well, as you see, I'm still alive and even highly prosperous.'

'Did you show them the Sainte-Chapelle?'

'They were in luck. It was just shutting, we just had time for a quick sprint past the stained-glass windows. Fabulous (gesture), anyway, the stained-glass windows. They're delighted (gesture) that lot. Aren't you, mia gretchen signora?'

The chosen lady tourist acquiesced, entranced.

'Hurrah!' cried the others.

'Stop, guidenappers,' added the widow Mouaque, Trouscaillon close on her heels.

The copman approached Gabriel and, bowing respectfully, inquired as to the state of his health. Gabriel replied succinctly that it was good. The other then pursued his interrogatory by broaching the problem of liberty. Gabriel reassured his interlocutor as to the extent of his own, which, what was more, he judged to be such as to meet his requirements. True, he did not deny that there had, at the outset, been an unquestionable attempt on his in this respect most imprescriptible rights, but, finally, once he had adjusted himself to the situation, he had transformed it to such an extent that his ravishers had become his slaves and that he would soon be in a position to dispose of their free will as he pleased. He added in conclusion that he strongly disliked the police coming and sticking its nose into his affairs and, since the horror which such actions inspired in him was not far from making him wish to vomit, he extracted from his pocket a silken square of the colour of the lilac flower (the one that isn't white) but impregnated with Barbouze, the Fior perfume, and with it dabbed his snitch.

Trouscaillon, stunk out, akscused himself, saluted Gabriel, bringing himself to attention, egzecuted the regulation about turn, withdrew, disappeared into the crowd accompanied by the widow Mouaque who followed close behind him at a gentle trot.

'You certainly put *him* in his place,' said Zazie to Gabriel, making room for herself at his side. 'I'll have a strawberry and chocolate ice.'

'Strikes me I've seen his face before somewhere,' said Gabriel.

'Now that we've got rid of the law,' said Zazie, 'perhaps you'll answer me. Are you a hormosessual or aren't you?'

'I swear I'm not.'

And Gabriel stretched out his hand and spat on the ground, which shocked the travellers somewhat. He was about to explain this feature of gallic folklore to them when Zazie, forestalling him in his didactic intentions, asked him why in that case the chap had accused him of being one.

'Here we go again,' groaned Gabriel.

The travellers, vaguely understanding, began to think that it wasn't the least bit funny any more, and took counsel with each other in low voices and in their native idioms. Some were for throwing the little girl into the Seine, others for wrapping her up in a travelling rug and depositing her in the left-luggage office of some station or other, having first stuffed her with cotton wool to render her insonorous. If nobody was willing to sacrifice a rug, a suitcase might answer the purpose, bit of a squeeze, though.

Uneasy about these confabulations, Gabriel decided to make a few concessions.

'Well,' he said, 'I'll explain all about it tonight. Better still, you'll see with your own eyes.'

'What'll I see?'

'You'll see. That's a promise.'

Zazie shrugged her shoulders.

'Oh promises, personally . . .'

'D'you want me to spit again?'

'Once is enough. You'll splash my ice-cream.'

'Right then now leave me in peace. You'll see, it's a promise.'

'What'll the little girl see?' asked Fyodor Balanovitch who had finally settled his collision with the Sanctimontronian who incidentally had manifested a strong inclination to disappear from the scene.

He now installed himself next to Gabriel and the travellers respectfully made room for him.

'I'm taking her to the Mount of Venus tonight,' replied Gabriel (gesture), 'and the others too.'

'Sta minute,' said Fyodor Balanovitch, 'that's not in the programme. I've got to put them to bed early, because they're supposed to leave tomorrow morning for Gibraltar, city of ancient parapets. Such is their itinerary.'

'In any case,' said Gabriel, 'they like the idea.'

'They don't realize what's in store for them,' said Fyodor Balanovitch.

'It'll be something for them to remember,' said Gabriel.

'Me too,' said Zazie, who was methodically carrying out various experiments on the comparative flavours of strawberry and chocolate.

'Yes but,' said Fyodor Balanovitch, 'who's going to pay at the Mount of Venus? They'll never stand for an extra charge.'

'I've got them well in hand,' said Gabriel.

'By the way,' said Zazie, 'I believe it's just coming back to me, the question I wanted to ask you.'

'Well it can wait,' said Fyodor Balanovitch. 'Pipe down, the men are speaking.'

Impressed, Zazie shut her trap.

As a waiter perchance was passing, Fyodor Balanovitch said to him:

'I'll have a beer juice.'

'In a mug or in the can?' asked the waiter.

'In a coffin,' replied Fyodor Balanovitch who made a sign to the waiter indicating that that would be all thank you.

'Oh that one's supreme,' Zazie made bold to say. 'Even General Vermot wouldn't have thought that one up all by himself.'

Fyodor Balanovitch pays not the slightest attention to the remarks of the junior doll.

'So you mean to say,' he asks Gabriel, 'you think we can swing a surcharge on 'em?'

'I tell you I've got them well in hand. Might as well make the most of it. Come to think of it, for egzample, where are you taking them for dinner?'

'Aha! they're getting properly looked after. They're entitled to the Buisson d'Argent. But it's paid directly by the agency.'

'Look. I know a brasserie in the Boulevard Turbigo where it'd cost far less. What you do is you go and see the boss of your luxury joint and you get him to give you back part of what he gets from the agency, it's all profit for all concerned and, what's more, in the place I'll take them to they'll have a terrific blow-out. Naturally we'll pay for that with the supplement that we'll ask them for the Mount of Venus. And the refund from the other joint, we'll divide that.'

'Artful little things, you two,' said Zazie.

'Now that,' said Gabriel, 'is just pure spite. Everything I do is for their (gesture) enjoyment.'

'That's all we think of,' said Fyodor Balanovitch. 'So's they'll go away with an unforgettable memory of this inclitic urb that's vocited Parish. So's they'll come back again.'

'Well then, everything's for the best,' said Gabriel. 'While they're waiting for dinner they can try out the brasserie's basement: fifteen billiard tables, twenty gnip-gnop. Unique in Paris.'

'It'll be something for them to remember,' said Fyodor Balano-vitch.

'Me too,' said Zazie. 'Because in the meantime, I shall go for a walk.'

'Not in the Boulevard Sébastopol, whatever you do,' said Gabriel in a panic.

'Don't worry,' said Fyodor Balanovitch, 'she certainly knows how to look after herself.'

'Even so her mother didn't leave her with me so's she should go trailing round between the Halles and the Château d'eau.'

'I'll just walk up and down in front of your brasserie,' said Zazie, trying to be helpful.

'All the more reason for people to think you're soliciting,' iksclaimed Gabriel, scared to death. 'Particularly with your blew-genes. There's specialists.'

'There's specialists in everything,' said Fyodor Balanovitch, very much the man of the world.

'You aren't being very nice to me,' said Zazie, wriggling.

'If she's going to start making eyes at you, now, that'll be the end.'

'Why?' asked Zazie. 'Is he a hormo?'

'You mean a normal,' Fyodor Balanovitch corrected her. 'Supreme, that one, isn't it unkoo?'

And he slapped Gabriel on the thigh. Gabriel fluttered. The travellers looked at them curiously.

'They must be getting bored,' said Fyodor Balanovitch. 'It's time you took them off to your billiard-saloon to entertain them an iota. Poor innocents who think that that's what Paris is.'

'You forget I showed them the Saint-Chapelle,' said Gabriel proudly.

'*Nigaud*,' said Fyodor Balanovitch, who had a thorough knowledge of the French language, being a native of Bois-Colombes. 'Noodle. That was the Commercial Court you took them round.'

'You're pulling my leg,' said Gabriel, incredulous. 'Are you sure?'

'Good thing Charles isn't here,' said Zazie. 'Things would get complicated.'

'If it wasn't the Sainte-Thingummy,' said Gabriel, 'at any rate it was very fine.'

'Sainte-Thingummy??? Sainte-Thingummy???' asked the most francophonic among the travellers, worried.

'The Sainte-Chapelle,' said Fyodor Balanovitch. 'That gem of Gothic art.'

'Fabulous (gesture),' added Gabriel.

Reassured, the travellers smiled.

'Well?' said Gabriel. 'Are you going to ksplain to them?'

Fyodor Balanovitch ciceroned the matter in several idioms.

'Well,' said Zazie, the complete connoisseur, 'he knows his onions, this Slav.'

All the more so as the travellers manifested their willingness by producing their cash with enthusiasm, thus bearing witness both to Gabriel's prestige and the extent of Fyodor Balanovitch's linguistic knowledge.

'Ah, that's what it was, my second question,' said Zazie. 'When I came across you at the bottom of the Eiffel Tower, you were talking foreign stuff as well as he does. What'd come over you? And why don't you go on doing it?'

'That,' said Gabriel, 'I can't esplain. It's just one of those things that happen, no one knows how. A touch of genius, eh.'

He finishes his glass of grenadine.

'There's nothing you can do about it, that's the way it is with artists.'

12

Trouscaillon and the widow Mouaque had already gone some way slowly side by side but straight ahead and furthermore in silence, when they observed that they were walking side by side but straight ahead and furthermore in silence. So they looked at one another and smiled: their two hearts had spoken. They remained face to face asking themselves what on earth they could say and in what language to express it. Then the widow suggested that they should there and then commemorate this encounter by draining a verre and that they should penetrate with this end in view into the café Vélocipède in the Boulevard Sébastopol, where several porters from the market were already moistening their ingestive tubes before carting their vegetables about. A marble table would offer them its plush-covered bench and they would dip their lips into their half-pints while they waited for the livid-fleshed waitress to withdraw so that at last some words of love might blossom through the bulbulating of their beers. At the hour when one is wont to drink soft drinks of strong colour and strong drinks of pale colour, they would stay put on the above-mentioned plush-covered bench exchanging, in the agitation of their intertwined hands, vocables prolific of sexualized observances in a not far distant future. But just a moment, replied Trouscaillon, I can't instanter, bellicause of my uniform; give me time to change my clobber. And he made a tryst with her for an aperitif at the Spheroid Brasserie, further up on the right. Because he lived in rue Rambuteau.

The widow Mouaque, solitary once more, sighed. I'm making a fool of myself, she said under her breath and to herself. But these few words fell not dully and ignored upon the pavement; they fell into the earholes of one who was anything but deaf. Destined for internal application, these six words nevertheless provoked the reply which you see here: who doesn't. With an interrogation point, for the reply was percontative.

'Oh, it's you,' said the widow Mouaque.

'I was watching you just now, you were killing, the two of you, you and the copman.'

'In your eyes,' said the widow Mouaque.

'"In my eyes"? How d'you mean "in my eyes"?'

'Killing,' said the widow Mouaque. 'To other eyes, not killing.'

'The not-killing,' said Zazie, 'make me puke.'

'Are you all by yourself?'

'Ja ja, my dear, I'm going for a walk.'

'It's neither the time nor the place to let a little girl go for a walk by herself. What's happened to your uncle?'

'He's carting the travellers around. He's taken them to play billiards. In the meantime, I'm taking the air. Because personally, billiards makes me puke. But I'm to meet them for grub. Afterwards, we're going to see him dance.'

'Dance? Who?'

'My unkoo.'

'Does he dance, that elephant?'

'And in a tutu, what's more,' retorted Zazie proudly.

The widow Mouaque was struck all of a heap.

They were now outside a grocer's, wholesale and retail; on the other side of the one-way boulevard a chemist's, no less wholesaling and no less retailing, was pouring its green lights over a crowd avid for camomile and pâté de campagne, for humbugs and semen-contra, for gruyère and cupping-glasses, a crowd which the suctorial proximity of the stations was anyway beginning to rarefy.

The widow Mouaque sighed.

'You don't mind if I walk with you a bit?'

'D'you want to keep an eye on me?'

'No, but you'd keep me company.'

'A lot I care about that. I'd rather be by myself.'

Once more the widow Mouaque sighed. 'And I'm so lonely . . . so lonely . . . so lonely . . .'

'Lonely my arse,' said the little girl with the propriety of language which was her wont.

'You ought to try and understand grown-ups, though,' said the lady in a watery voice. 'Ah! if you only knew . . .'

'Is it the copman who's got you in such a state?'

'Ah, love . . . when you know . . .'

'I knew it, I was just telling myself that all you really wanted was to come out with a lot of filth. If you don't shut up I'll call a cop . . . a different one . . .'

'How cruel,' said the widow Mouaque bitterly.

Zazie shrugged her shoulders.

'Poor old thing . . . Come on now, I'm not such a bad sort. I'll keep you company till you've pulled yourself together. Warm-hearted, aren't I?'

Before the old Mouaque a dad time to answer, Zazie had added:

'All the same . . . a copper. Couldn't stomach that myself.'

'I know what you mean. But well, what could I do, it just happened that way. Perhaps if your uncle hadn't been guidenapped . . .'

'I've already told you he's married. And my aunt's a hell of a lot better-looking than you are.'

'You don't need to advertise your family. My Trouscaillon is good enough for me. Will be good enough for me, that is.'

Zazie shrugged her shoulders.

'All this stuff comes straight out of the movies,' said she. 'You wouldn't have another subject of conversation?'

'No,' said the widow Mouaque energetically.

'In that case,' said Zazie no less energetically, 'I wish to state that courtesy week is over. 'Bye.'

'Thank you all the same, my child,' said the widow Mouaque, full of indulgence.

They crossed the road together separately and met again in front of the Spheroid Brasserie.

'Well well,' said Zazie, 'here you are again. Are you following me?'

'I would prefer to see you elsewhere,' said the widow.

'Oh now that one's supreme. Lessen five minutes ago *you* couldn't be got rid of. Now *I'*m to take a walk. Is it love that makes people like that?'

'Oh well you know. If you *must* know, I have a date right here with my Trouscaillon.'

From the basement there emanated a great brou. Ha ha.

'So have I with my unkoo,' said Zazie. 'They're all there. Down below. Hear them romping around? They're pre-historic. Because, as I told you, to me, billiards . . .'

The widow Mouaque was conning the contents of the ground floor.

'He's not there, your boyo,' said Zazie.

'Notchette,' said the lady. 'Notchette.'

'Course he isn't. There never are any cops in bistros. It's not allowed.'

'That,' said the widow delicately, 'is where you're buggered. He's gone to put his civvies on.'

'And you reckon you'll recognize him when he looks civilized?'

'I love him,' said the widow Mouaque.

'In the meantime,' said Zazie good-naturedly, 'why don't you come down and have a drink with us. He may be in the basement, after all. Perhaps he did it on purrpuss.'

'Don't need to egzaggerate. He's a cop, not a spy.'

'How do you know? Has he taken you into his confidence? Already?'

'I have faith,' said the old trout, no less ecstatically than enigmatically.

Zazie shrugged her shoulders once again.

'Come on . . . a drink, that'll give you something else to think about.'

'Why not,' said the widow who had looked at the time and had just realised that she still had ten minutes to wait for her copulo.

From the top of the staircase, little balls could be seen gliding briskly along green cloths and other, lighter ones were zebra-striping the mist that was rising from half-pints of beer and moist braces. Zazie and the widow Mouaque spotted the compact group of travellers aggregated round Gabriel, who was meditating a carom of extreme difficulty. Having brought it off he was acclaimed in different idioms.

'They seem pleased, eh,' said Zazie, very proud of her unkoo.

The lady, with her noddle, appeared to agree.

'Fantastic what bloody asses they are,' Zazie added tenderly. 'And they haven't seen anything yet. When Gabriel comes on in a tutu, what're they going to look like then.'

The lady deigned to smile.

'What exactly is it, a fairy?' Zazie asked her affably, as woman to woman. 'A pansy? a queen? a pederast? a hormosessual? Are there little differences?'

'My poor child,' said, sighing, the widow who from time to time rediscovered some fragments of morality to apply to other people in the ruins of her own which had been pulverized by the charms of the copman.

Gabriel, who had just made a balls of a six-cushion push stroke, noticed them at that moment and gave them a friendly wave. Then he coldly resumed his break, ignoring the failure of his previous carom.

'I'm going back up,' said the widow decisively.

'Happy hunting,' said Zazie, and she went to watch the billiards from closer to.

The cue ball was in f2, the other white ball in g3 and the red in h4. Gabriel was preparing himself for a massé shot and, with this end in view, was chalking his cue. He said:

'Doesn't seem possible to get rid of her, that old trout.'

'She's got a tremendous thing about the copman, the one who spoke to you when we came into the bistro.'

'Who cares. For the moment, just let me play this game. No funny stuff. Ts have some peace. Some sang-froid.'

In the midst of general admiration, he lifted his cue in the air and then struck the cue ball sharply, in order to cause it to describe a parabolic curve. He made a stroke which, deviating from its precise application, went on to slash the cloth with a zebra stripe which represented a specific market value computed by the bosses of the establishment. The travellers who, on neighbouring devices, had been attempting unsuccessfully to produce a similar result, gave vent to their admiration. It was time to have dinner. After he'd taken round the hat to pay the expenses and settled the bill equitably, Gabriel, having retrieved his flock, including the gnip-gnop players, led them off to have their grub at street level. The brasserie on the ground floor seemed to him to be appropriate to this enterprise, and he had flung himself down on a bench before he saw the widow Mouaque and Trouscaillon at a table opposite. They waved to him merrily, and Gabriel had difficulty in recognizing the copman in the gent in his Sunday best who was simpering by the side of the old trout. Turning a deaf ear to everything but the intermittencies of his kind heart, Gabriel by means of a gesture bade them join his retinue, which bidding did not go unheeded. The foreigners choked with enthusiasm at so much local colour, while the waiters dressed in loinclothes started to serve, to the accompaniment of half-pints of rheumy beer, a filthy Sauerkraut studded with bready sausages, mouldy bacon, leathery ham and germinating potatoes, thus presenting for the ill-considered appreciation of well-disposed palates the ffine efflorescence of the ffrensh cuisine.

Zazie, testing the viands, declared quite bluntly that they were squit. The copman, who had been brought up by his mother, a concierge, in a solid tradition of yesterday's beef rehashed in onion sauce, the old troutess, an expert at authentic fried spuds, even Gabriel himself, although accustomed to the strange sustenance served in cabarets, lost no time in suggesting to the child that cowardly silence which allows lousy hash-and-slop producers to corrupt the public taste on the level of internal politics and, on the level of external politics, to debase in the eyes of foreigners the magnificent heritage handed down to the kitchen of France from the Gauls to whom we owe, in addition, as everyone knows, breeches, cooperage and abstract art.

'All the same you can't stop me saying,' said Zazie, 'that it (gesture) 's muck.'

'Course not, course not,' said Gabriel, 'I don't want to force you. I'm understanding, aren't I, madame?'

'Sometimes,' said the widow Mouaque. 'Sometimes.'

'It's not that so much,' said Trouscaillon, 'it's a question of courtesy.'

'Courtesy my arse,' said Zazie.

'You,' said Gabriel to the copman, 'are kindly requested to allow me to bring up this kid as I think best. *I* have the responsibilitas for her. Don't I, Zazie?'

'Seems so,' said Zazie.'In any case, personally, nothing's going to make me swallow this filth.'

'What would mademoiselle like?' hypocritically enquired a vicious waiter who smelt a brawl.

'I want summingelse,' said Zazie.

'Doesn't the little lady like our alsatian sauerkraut?' asked the vicious waiter.

He was trying to be ironical, the silly bastard.

'No,' said Gabriel with vigour and authority, 'she doesn't like it.'

The waiter considered Gabriel's format for a few moments and then, in Trouscaillon, he caught a whiff of the cop. So many trumps united in the single hand of a little girl induced him to shut his great gob. He was all set, therefore, to give a demonstration of arse-licking, when a manager, an even sillier bastard, took it into his head to intervene. He forthwith switched on his charm act.

'Oy oy, oy oy,' he oyed, 'foreigners taking the liberty of talking about cooking? Well bloody hell, they've got a cheek, tourists, this year. Maybe they're going to start claiming they know something about grub, the dumbclucks.'

He addressed some few of their number (gestures).

'No but really look here, so you imagine we fought several victorious wars just for you to come and spit on our bombes glacées? You think we cultivate our red wine and methylated spirits with the sweat of our brows just for you to come and abuse them in aid of your filthy cocacola and chianti? You lotus-eating lot, while you were still practising cannibalism, sucking the marrow from the bones of your butchered enemies, our ancestors the Crusaders were already cooking steak and fried potatoes even before Parmentier discovered the potato, not to mention black pudding with french beans which you've never yet had the intelligence to fabricate. You don't like it? Eh? As if you knew the first thing about it!'

He took another breath and continued in these courteous terms:

'Maybe it's the prices that make you look like that? They're more than fair, though, our prices are. You don't realize, you tight-arsed lot. What would he not pay his taxes with, the boss, if he didn't take into consideration all your dollars you don't know what to do with.'

'Finished talking crap?' asked Gabriel.

The manager utters a cry of rage.

'What's more they think they can talk French,' he started howling.

He turned to the vicious waiter and communicated his impressions to him:

'No really though d'you hear this vulgar shit-hound who makes so bold as to address me in our dialect. If that isn't the most nauseating . . .'

'Doesn't speak so badly though,' said the vicious waiter, who was afraid of being beaten up.

'Traitor,' said the manager exacerbated, haggard and tremulous.

'What're you waiting for, why don't you bash his face in?' Zazie asked Gabriel.

'Shh,' said Gabriel.

'Twist his private parts for him,' said the widow Mouaque, 'that'll teach him.'

'I don't want to see that,' said Trouscaillon, who had turned green. 'While you're carrying out the operation I'll absent myself for the requisite time. I've just got to go and give the copshop a buzz.'

The vicious waiter nudged the manager in the tum to underline the customer's remark. The wind changed.

'Well after all that,' the manager began, 'after all that, what would mademoiselle like?'

'The stuff you gave me,' said Zazie, 'is just plain squit.'

'They made a mistake,' said the manager, with a kindly smile, 'they made a mistake, that was for the next table, for the travellers.'

'They're with us,' said Gabriel.

'Don't worry,' said the manager with a collusive air. 'I'll be able to find another customer for my sauerkraut all right. What would you like instead, mademoiselle?'

'Another sauerkraut.'

'Another sauerkraut?'

'Yes,' said Zazie, 'another sauerkraut.'

'The thing is,' said the manager, 'the other won't be any better than this one. I'm telling you straight out so's you don't start complaining all over again.'

'In short, there's nothing but muck to eat in your establishment?'

'At your service,' said the manager. 'Ah, if there weren't any taxes (sigh).'

'Yum yum,' said a traveller as he polished off his last scrap of sauerkraut. He intimated with a gesture that he wanted some more.

'There you are,' said the manager triumphantly.

And Zazie's plate, which the vicious waiter had just taken away, reappeared in front of the bulimic traveller.

'I can see you're connoisseurs,' continued the manager, 'so I should advise you to have our plain corned beef. And I'll open the tin in front of you.'

'It took him long enough to understand,' said Zazie.

Humiliated, the other withdrew. Gabriel, the good soul, wanting to cheer him up, asked:

'What about your grenadine? Is your grenadine any good?'

13

Mado Ptits-pieds watched the telephone ring for three seconds, then at the fourth, addressed herself to the task of listening to what was going on at the other end. She took the instrument off its perch and heard it forthwith assume Gabriel's voice and inform her that he had a couple of words to say to his ever-loving.

'And get cracking,' it added.

'Can't,' said Mado Ptits-pieds, 'I'm on my own, msieu Turandot isn't here.'

'Talk,' said Laverdure, 'talk, that's all you can do.'

'Well clotess,' said Gabriel's voice, 'if there's no one there you can lock the door, and if there is someone you can sling him out. Got it, dim-wit?'

'Yes, msieu Gabriel.'

And she hung up. It wasn't so simple. There was in fact a customer. She could have left him on his own, at that, since it was Charles and since Charles wasn't the type to go ferreting around in the till in order to possess himself of some few pieces of currency. A decent chap, Charles. As proved by the fact that he had just proposed holy wedlock to her.

Mado Ptits-pieds had hardly begun to ponder this problem when the telephone started to ring again.

'Hell,' roared Charles, 'no way of getting a bit of peace in this brothel.'

'Talk, talk,' said Laverdure whom the situation was irritating, 'that's all you can do.'

Mado Ptits-pieds took the receiver into her hands once more and heard propelled in her direction a certain number of adjectives, one more disagreeable than the other.

'Don't hang up you hag, you wouldn't know where to call me back. And get a move on, dammit, are you by yourself or is there someone there?'

'ZCharles.'

'What is desired of Charles?' said Charles nobly.

'Talk, talk, that's all,' said Laverdure, 'you can do.'

'Is it Charles making that row?' asked the telephone.

'No, that's Laverdure. Charles – Charles is talking wedding bells.'

'Ah! he's made up his mind,' said the telephone indifferently. 'Doesn't stop him going and fetching Marceline, if you don't want to strain yourself, what with the stairs. He'd certainly do that for you, old Charles would.'

'I'll go a nask him,' said Mado Ptits-pieds.

(a pause)

'He says he duh wantoo.'

'Why?'

'He's cross with you.'

'Silly bugger. Tell him to get on the line.'

'Charles,' called Mado Ptits-pieds (gesture).

Charles doesn't say anything (gesture).

Mado gets impatient (gesture).

'Well is he coming?' asks the telephone.

'Yes,' says Mado Ptits-pieds (gesture).

Finally Charles empties his glass and slowly approaches the receiver, then, snatching the instrument from the hands of his perhaps intended, he utters the cybernetic word:

'Hallo.'

'Zthat you, Charles?'

'Grrr.'

'Well then get cracking and go and fetch Marceline so's I can talk to her, it surgeont.'

'I don't take orders from anyone.'

'Oh blimey, tsnothing to do with that, I tell you get a jerk on, it surgeont.'

'And *I* tell *you* that I don't take orders from anyone.'

And he hangs up.

Then he went back to the counter behind which Mado Ptits-pieds seemed to be dreaming.

'Well,' said Charles, 'what d'you think? Is it yes is it no?'

'I've already told you,' whispered Mado Ptits-pieds, 'you say that like that, without any warning, tsa shock, I hadn't expected it, it'll need thinking over, msieu Charles.'

'As if you hadn't already thought it over.'

'Oh! msieu Charles, you are skeleptical.'

The ringing of the whatsit-thing started to telefunction all over again.

'Oh look here what's the matter with him, what's the matter with him.'

'Just don't answer it,' said Charles.

'Don't need to be so hard-hearted, after all he's a pal.'

'Yerss, but with the brat thrown in it doesn't exactly help.'

'Forget about the kid. At that age it doesn't mean a thing.'

As the thing went on whirring, Charles again placed himself at the end of the line of the unhooked instrument.

'Hallo,' roared Gabriel.

'Grrr,' said Charles.

'Oh come on, don't arse around. Go on, get going and fetch Marceline and you're beginning to make me sick now I come to think of it.'

'You don't seem to understand,' said Charles in a superior tone of voice, 'you're disturbing me.'

'Well Ida know,' bellowed the telephone, 'what next. Disturbing you. You. What the devil can you be doing that's so important?'

Charles energetically placed his hand on the instrument's fonator and, turning to Mado, asked her:

'Zit yes? rizit no?'

'Ts yes,' replied Mado Ptits-pieds, blushing.

'Really and truly?'

'(gesture).'

Charles unblocked the fonator and communicated the following information to Gabriel still present at the other end of the line.

'Well it's like this, I've got some news for you.'

'To hell with your news. Go and fetch . . .'

'Marceline, I know.'

Then he rushes in, full speed ahead:

'Mado Ptits-pieds and me, we've just got engaged.'

'Good idea. After all, I've been thinking, you don't need to bother . . .'

'Did you understand what I said? Mado Ptits-pieds and me, it's wedding bells.'

'If that's the way you feel. Yes, Marceline, don't bother to disturb her. Just tell her that I'm taking the kid to the Mount of Venus to see the show. I've got some distinguished travellers with me and a few pals, quite a crowd, eh. So my act, well, tonight I'm going to take some trouble over it. Zazie might as well take advantage of it, it's a real piece of luck for her. Huh, that's an idea, why don't you come too, bring Mado Ptits-pieds, to celebrate your engagement, what d'you say, eh? Have to drink to it, a thing like that, I'll pay, and for the show as well. And then Turandot, he can come too, the mutt, and Laverdure if anyone thinks it'll amuse him, and Gridoux, mustn't forget him, Gridoux. Good old Gridoux.'

Whereupon Gabriel hangs up.

Charles lets the receiver swing on the end of its cord, turns to Mado Ptits-pieds and addresses himself to the task of enunciating something memorable.

'Well,' says he, 'so that's that, is it? It's in the bag?'

'And how,' says Madeleine.

'We're going to get married, me and Madeleine,' said Charles to Turandot who was just reappearing.

'Good idea,' said Turandot. 'I'll stand you a pick-me-up to celebrate. But I don't like the idea of losing Mado. She worked well.'

'Yes but well I'll be staying on,' said Madeleine. 'I'd be bored stiff at home, while he's doing his taxi-ing.'

'Yes that's true,' said Charles. 'After all, nothing'll be different, except that when we have a bit it'll be within the four corners of the law.'

'People always end up by making the best of things,' said Turandot. 'What'll you have?'

'Oh I don't care,' said Charles.

'Just for once *I*'ll serve *you*,' said Turandot to Madeleine gallantly, patting her on the bottom, which he wasn't in the habit of doing outside working hours and then only to warm up the atmosphere.

'Charles, he might have a Fernet-Branca,' said Madeleine.

'It's undrinkable,' said Charles.

'You managed a glass at lunchtime all right,' Turandot observed.

'So I did, that's true. Then I'll have a beaujolais.'

They touch glasses.

'To your legitimate nookies,' said Turandot.

'Thanks,' replies Charles, wiping his mouth with his cap.

He adds that there's another thing, he's got to go and tell Marceline.

'Don't you bother, sweetie,' says Madeleine, 'I'll go.'

'What the hell does she care whether you get married or not?' said Turandot. 'She can easily wait till tomorrow to be told.'

'Marceline,' said Charles, 'that's another matter. It's that Gabriel's still got Zazie with him and he's inviting us all and you too to come and have one and watch him do his act. Have one and I sincerely hope several.'

'Well,' said Turandot, 'nothing squeamish about you. Going to go to a pansy nightclub to celebrate your engagement? Well, as I said, nothing squeamish about you.'

'Talk, talk,' said Laverdure, 'that's all you can do.'

'Don't quarrel,' said Madeleine. 'I'll go and tell madame Marceline and then dress myself up posh to be a credit to our Gaby.'

She takes wing. The second floor arrived at, the doorbell is rung by the new fiancée. A door rung at in so gracious a fashion cannot but open. Thus the door in question opens.

'Hallo, Mado Ptits-pieds,' said Marceline gently.

'Well it's like this,' said Madeleine, getting back the breath she'd scattered more or less at random in the helices of the staircase.

'Come in and have a glass of grenadine,' said Marceline gently, interrupting her.

'The thing is I've got to get dressed.'

'You don't look naked to me,' said Marceline gently.

Madeleine blushed. Marceline said gently:

'And that doesn't stop us having a glass of grenadine, does it?
Just us women . . .'

'All the same.'

'You look quite upset.'

'Vjust got engaged. So you see . . .'

'You aren't pregnant?'

'Not for the moment.'

'Then you can't refuse to let me offer you a glass of grenadine.'

'Oo you do talk nicely.'

'It's really not my doing,' said Marceline gently, lowering her
eyes. 'Do come in.'

Madeleine murmurs some more embarrassed civilities and enters.
Invited to sit down, she does so. The mistress of the house goes to
procure two glasses, a carafe of aitchtwowoh and a litre of grenadine.
She pours this latter liquid with care, fairly generously for her guest,
just a thimbleful for herself.

'I have to be careful,' she says gently, with a conspiratorial smile.

Then she dilutes the beverage, which they sip affectedly.

'Well? asks Marceline gently.

'Well then,' says Madeleine, 'meussieu Gabriel phoned that he's
taking Zazie to his joint to see his act, and us two as well, Charles
and me, to celebrate our engagement.'

'Because it's Charles?'

'Might as well be him as anyone else. You can rely on him, and
anyway we know each other.'

They continued to smile at each other.

'Tell me, madame Marceline,' says Madeleine, 'what sort of get-up
ought I to have?'

'Wurll,' said Marceline gently, 'for an engagement, medium-white
is indispensable, with a touch of virginal silver.'

'You can forget the virginal part,' said Madeleine.

'That's what's done.'

'Even in a pansy joint?'

'That has nothing to do with it.'

'Yes but yes but yes but, supposing I haven't got a medium-white
dress with a touch of virginal silver, or even a bath-room two-piece

tailor-made with a kitchen jumper suspender-belt, well then, what do I do? No but tell me just tell me, what do I do?'

Marceline bowed her head thus showing the most manifest signs of thought.

'Well,' said she gently, 'well in that case why don't you wear your purple jacket with the green and yellow pleated skirt that I saw you in one day when there was dancing, one fourteenth of July.'

'You noticed it?'

'Of course,' said Marceline gently, 'I noticed it (silence). You were enchanting.'

'Oh that is nice,' said Madeleine. 'So just like that you notice me, now and then?'

'Of course I do,' said Marceline gently.

'Cos what I think,' said Madeleine, 'cos I think you're so beautiful.'

'Really?' asked Marceline with gentleness.

'I should just think I do,' replied Mado with vehemence, 'I should certainly think I do. You're simply terrific. Wouldn't I just like to be like you. You've got such a marvellous figure. And so elegant and all.'

'Don't let's exaggerate,' said Marceline gently.

'Oh but you are you are, you're simply terrific. Why don't we see you more often? (silence). We'd like to see you more often. I (smile) 'd like to see you more often.'

Marceline lowered her eyes and gently turned pink.

'Yes,' Madeleine went on, 'why don't we see you more often, you who are in such radiant good health that I take the liberty of drawing your attention to it and so beautiful into the bargain, yes why?'

'The thing is I'm not the flashy type,' replied Marceline gently.

'Without going as far as that, you could . . .'

'Let's just leave it at that, my dear,' said Marceline.

Whereupon they remained silent, thoughtful, dreamy. Time did not flow rapidly for the two of them. They heard from afar, in the streets, tyres slowly deflating in the night. Through the open window they saw the moon scintillating on the antennae of a telly aerial and making only very little noise about it.

'All the same you ought to go and get dressed,' said Marceline gently, 'if you don't want to miss Gabriel's act.'

'Yes I must,' said Madeleine. 'So I put on my apple-green jacket with the orange and lemon fourteenth of July skirt?'

'That's it.'

(a pause)

'Just the same, it makes me sad to leave you all by yourself.'

'Oh no,' said Marceline. 'I'm used to it.'

'Just the same.'

They stood up together with a simultaneous impulse.

'Oh well, if that's the way it is,' said Madeleine, 'I'll go and get dressed.'

'You'll be enchanting,' said Marceline, gently approaching her.

Madeleine looks into her eyes.

There's a knock at the door.

'Well are you coming?' yells Charles.

14

The jalopy filled up and Charles drove off. Turandot sat beside him, Madeleine in the back between Gridoux and Laverdure.

Madeleine studied the parrot and then asked the assembled company:

'D'you think he'll enjoy the show?'

'Don't worry,' said Turandot who had pushed back the glass partition to hear what might be said behind him, 'you know perfectly well he enjoys himself in his own way, when he feels like it. So why not by watching Gabriel?'

'With these creatures,' declared Gridoux, 'you never know what's going on in their heads.'

'Talk, talk,' said Laverdure, 'that's all you can do.'

'You see,' said Gridoux, 'they understand more than most people think.'

'That's true enough,' agreed Madeleine with enthusiasm. 'That's absolutely true. Anyway what about us, do we really understand anything about anything?'

'Anything about what?' asked Turandot.

'About life. Sometimes you might think it was a dream.'

'People always talk like that when they're going to get married.'

And Turandot gives Charles' thigh a sonorous clip thus running the risk of the taxi turning a Charlesault.

'Don't be so damn silly,' says Charles.

'No,' says Madeleine, 'it's not that, I wasn't only thinking about the wedding bells, I was just thinking, that's all.'

'That's the only way,' said Gridoux in an authoritative tone.

'The only way to do what?'

'What you said.'

(silence)

'What a stinking lousy life,' went on Madeleine (sigh).

'Oh no,' said Gridoux, 'oh no.'

'Talk, talk,' said Laverdure, 'that's all you can do.'

'Well Ida know,' said Gridoux, 'he doesn't often change his tune, that thing.'

'Are you insinuating that he's not gifted?' shouted Turandot over his shoulder.

Charles, whom Laverdure had never very much interested, leant over to his owner and said under his breath:

'Ask if it's still on, the wedding bells.'

'Who do I ask? Laverdure?'

'Don't be more of a dope than you have to.'

'Can't even crack a joke any more, it seems,' said Turandot in an emollient voice.

And he called over his shoulder:

'Mado Ptits-pieds!'

'Coming,' said Madeleine.

'Charles wants to know if you still want him for your lawful wedded husband.'

'I dooo,' replied Madeleine in a steady voice.

Turandot turned to Charles and asked him:

'Do you still want Mado Ptits-pieds for your lawful wedded wife?'

'I dooo,' replied Charles in a steady voice.

'Well then' said Turandot in a no less steady voice, 'I pronounce that you be Man and Wife together.'

'Amen,' said Gridoux.

'That's idiotic,' said Madeleine, furious, 'that's an idiotic joke.'

'Why?' asked Turandot. 'Do you want to or don't you want to? Have to make your minds up.'

'It was the joke that wasn't funny.'

'I wasn't joking. I've wanted to see you married for a long time, you and Charles.'

'Mind your own buttocks, msieu Turandot.'

'She had the last word,' said Charles calmly. 'Here we are. All change. I'll go and park my cab, I'll be back.'

'Just as well,' said Turandot, 'I was beginning to get a stiff neck. You're not cross with me?'

'Of course not,' said Madeleine, 'you're much too much of an ass for anyone to be cross with you.'

An admiral in ceremonial dress came to open the cab doors.

He gave tongue.

'Oh the little sweety,' said he, as he noticed the parrot. 'Is she one of us too?'

Laverdure protested:

'Talk, talk, that's all you can do.'

'Well well,' said the admiral, 'it looks as if she'd like a bit.'

And to the newcomers:

'You're Gabriella's guests? You could see that with half an eye.'

'Just a minute eh Miss Molly,' said Turandot, 'don't be cheeky.'

'And that, does that thing want to see Gabriella too?'

He studied the parrot and looked as if he looked as if he were about to vomit in disgust.

'Any objections?' demanded Turandot.

'Well, in a way,' replied the admiral. 'That kind of beastie gives me complexes.'

'Yought to see a psittaco-analyst,' said Gridoux.

'I *have* tried to analyse my dreams,' replied the admiral, 'but they're lousy. Can't get anything out of 'em.'

'What d'you dream about?' asked Gridoux.

'Wet-nurses.'

'What a dirty girl,' said Turandot, wanting to have his little joke. Charles had found a place to park his crate.

'What's going on,' said Charles, 'haven't you gone in yet?'

'Oo what a saucy girl,' said the admiral.

'I don't care for such jests,' said the taximann.

'I'll make a note of it,' said the admiral.

'Talk, talk,' said Laverdure . . .

'Infernal racket you're making,' said Gabriel, who'd materialized. 'Come on in. Don't be bashful. The customers haven't arrived yet.

Zonly the travellers. And Zazie. Come on in. Come on in. Any minute now you're going to be splitting your sides.'

'Why did you specially tell us to come this evening?' asked Turandot.

'You who,' Gridoux went on, 'used to throw the chaste veil of ostracism over the circumscription of your activities.'

'And whom,' added Madeleine, 'had always given us to understand that were we to come and admire you in the exercise of your art you wouldn't like it.'

'Yes,' said Laverdure, 'we neither understand the hic of this nunc nor the quid of this quod.'

Ignoring the parrot's intervention, Gabriel replied in these terms to his previous interlocutors:

'Why? You ask me why? Ah, strange question, when one knows neither what nor which to answer. Why? Yes, why? You ask me why? Oh! give me leave, in this sweet moment, to evoke that fusion of existence and of the almost why that is wrought in the crucibles of hypothecation and deposits. Why why why, you ask me why? Well, do you not hear the gloxinias quivering alongside the epithalamia?'

'Are you saying all that for our benefit?' asked Charles who often did cross-word puzzles.

'No, not in the least,' replied Gabriel. 'But look! look!'

A red-velvet curtain magically divided itself along a median line, revealing to the eyes of the wonder-struck visitors the bar, the tables, the platform and the dance floor of the Mount of Venus, the most celebrated of all the pansy night-clubs of the capital, and there's certainly no serious shortage of them, at this hour still only and feebly animated by the aberrant and slightly abnormal presence of the disciples of the cicerone Gabriel, in the middle of whom sat, enthroned and perorating, Childe Zazie.

'Make room, noble strangers,' said Gabriel.

Having complete confidence in him, they budged up to allow the newcomers to insert themselves in their midst. When they were all satisfactorily shuffled, they installed Laverdure on a table. He demonstrated his satisfaction by distributing sunflower seeds all around him.

A Scotch lassie, an ordinary waiter attached to the establishment, studied this character and communicated his opinion out loud.

'Certainly are some screwy people around. Personally, green pastures . . .'

'Great big poof,' said Turandot. 'If you think you're in your right mind, you and your fancy skirt.'

'Let him be,' said Gabriel, 'it's the tool of his trade. As for Laverdure,' he added, to the Scotch lassie, '*I* told him to come, so you can shut your great gob and keep your observations to your own sweet self.'

'That's really talking,' said Turandot, looking askance and victoriously at the Scotch lassie. 'Besiding which,' he added, 'what're they going to give us? Champagne, or what?'

'It's obligatory here,' said the Scotch lassie. 'Unless you have whisky. If you know what that is.'

'He yasks *me*,' exclaimed Turandot, 'me that's in the trade!'

'Should've said so,' said the Scotch lassie, dusting off his skirt with the back of his hand.

'Well, get going,' said Gabriel, 'bring us the gaseous swill of this establishment.'

'How many bottles?'

'That depends on the price,' said Turandot.

'I tell you this is on me,' said Gabriel.

'I was looking after your interests,' said Turandot.

'Isn't she a meanie,' said the Scotch lassie, tweaking the café-owner's ear and retiring forthwith. 'I'll bring a gross.'

'A gross what?' asked Zazie, suddenly taking an interest in the conversation.

'He means a dozen dozen bottles,' explained Gabriel, who does things on a grand scale.

Zazie then deigned to turn her attention to the newcomers.

'Well, taximan,' says she to Charles, 'seems we're getting married?'

'Seems so,' replied Charles succinctly.

'So you finally found someone that suits you.'

Zazie leant over and looked at Madeleine.

'Is it her?'

'Good evening mademoiselle,' said Madeleine, amiably.

'Hi,' said Zazie.

She turned to the widow Mouaque to put her in the picsh.

'Those two,' she tells her, pointing to the persons concerned, 'they're getting married.'

'Oh! how thrilling,' ksclaimed the widow Mouaque. 'And my poor Trouscaillon who is perhaps this very moment getting himself beaten up, on this dark night. Ah well (sigh), it's the profession he chose (silence). It would be comic if I were widowed a second time before I'd even got married.'

She gave a shrill little laugh.

'Who's the nutess?' Turandot asked Gabriel.

'Dunno. She's been sticking to us like a leech since the safternoon with a cop she picked up en route.'

'Which one's the cop?'

'He's gone for a blow.'

'I don't care for this company,' said Charles.

'Yes,' said Turandot, 'Tsnot healthy.'

'Neh mind,' said Gabriel. 'You don't want to worry about a little thing like that. Look, here comes the swill. Hurrah! Drench yourselves, friends and travellers, and you, dear niece, and you, fond fiancés. Good lord yes! Musn't forget them, the fiancés. A toast! A toast to the fiancés!'

The travellers, touched, sang *apibeursdé touillou* in chorus and a few Scotch lassie waiters, deeply moved, repress'd the starting tear that would have mucked up their mascara.

Then Gabriel tapped on a glass with a fizz-extractor, immediately secured the general attention, for such was his prestige, sat down back to front on a chair, and said:

'Well, my lambs and you my lady sheep, you are at last about to have a glimpse of my talents. For a long time indeed you have known, and some few among you have recently ceased to be unaware of the fact, that I have made of the choreographic art the principle pap of the udder of my revenue. One must live, must one not? And on what does one live? I ask you. On air, of course – at least partly, shall I say, and one dies of it too – but more fundamentally on that substantific marrow known as lolly. This mellifluent, sapid and polygenic product evaporates with the greatest facility, while it is only acquired by the sweat of one's brow at least among the iksploited of this world of whom I am one and the first of whom was named Adam who was persecuted by the Elohim as everyone knows. Although his situation in Eden wouldn't be regarded as specially costly to them in the eyes and according to the judgment of present-day human beings, they sent him to the colonies to lard the lean earth to make the grapefruit grow there at the same time as they refused to allow hypnotists to assist his spouse in her confinements and obliged the ophidians to sling their hook. Bibble-babble, bagatelles and biblicisms, and such-like crap. Be that as it may I have anointed my knee-joints with the aforementioned sweat of my brow and it is thus that as an edenite and adamite I earn my daily bread. You are to see me in action in a few moments but beware! make no mistake, it is no mere slip-tease that I shall offer you but art! Art with a capital a, mark it well! *De l'art* in four letters, and French four-letter words are incontestably superior both to the three-letter words which wash down so many vulgarities into the majestic current of the French language, and to the five-letter words which convey no less. Having reached the conclusion of my discourse it only remains for me to give expression to all my gratitude and all my gratefulness for the boundless applause with which you are about to make the welkin ring in my honour and to my greater glory. Thank you! In advance, thank you! Once again, thank you!'

And, springing to his feet with a suppleness as singular as it was unexpected, the colossus performed several entrechats, flapping his hands up and down behind his shoulder-blades in imitation of the flight of the butterfly.

This glimpse of his talent created considerable enthusiasm among the travellers.

'Geh, girl,' they cried, to encourage him.

'Gowit,' yelled Turandot, who had never drunk such good swill.

'Oh! the noisy girl,' said a Scotch lassie waiter.

While more customers were being deposited in clusters by the coaches that were such a familiar sight in these parts, Gabriel suddenly sat down again with a baleful air.

'Is anything wrong, meussieu Gabriel?' Madeleine asked kindly.

'I've got stage-fright.'

'Ape,' said Charles.

'Just my luck,' said Zazie.

'You wouldn't do that to us,' said Turandot.

'Talk, talk,' said Laverdure, 'that's all you can do.'

'She knows what she's talking about, does that wee sleekit beastie,' said a Scotch lassie waiter.

'Don't let us get you down, Gaby,' said Turandot.

'Just pretend we're the same as anyone else,' said Zazie.

'Just to please me,' said the widow Mouaque, simpering.

'You,' said Gabriel, 'be buggered. No, my friends,' he added, addressing himself to the others, 'no, it isn't only that (sigh) (silence), but I'd have liked it so much if Marceline could have been here to admire me too.'

It was then announced that the show was about to begin with a caromba danced by the sweetest little Martiniquians you ever saw.

15

Marceline had fallen asleep in an armchair. Something woke her up. Blinking, she looked at the time, drew no special conclusion therefrom, and finally realised that someone was very discreetly knocking at the door.

She immediately put out the light, and then didn't move. It couldn't be Gabriel because when he came home with the others they would naturally make enough row to wake up the whole neighbourhood. It wasn't the police either, seeing that the sun had not yet risen. As for the hypothesis that some marauder might covet Gabriel's savings, that rather inclined one to mirth.

There was a silence, and then someone started to turn the doorhandle. This giving no result, whoever it was started to mess about with the lock. This went on for some time. He's not very bright, said Marceline to herself. Finally the door opened.

The chap didn't come in straight away. Marceline was breathing so softly and artfully that he probably couldn't hear her.

At last he took a step. He was fumbling about, searching for the light switch. He managed to find it, and there was light in the hall.

Marceline immediately recognized the silhouette of the chap: it was the self-styled Pedro-surplus. But when he'd switched the light on in the room where she was sitting, Marceline thought she'd made a mistake because the individual she saw was wearing neither handle-bars nor dark glasses.

He was carrying his shoes in his hand, and smiling.

'I gave you the squitters, eh?' he asked gallantly.

'Nay,' replied Marceline gently.

He had sat down, and while he was silently putting his shoeshoes back on, she perceived that she had not been mistaken in her first identification. It was the chap Gabriel had thrown downstairs all right.

When he was shod, he again looked at Marceline and smiled.

'This time,' said he, 'I wouldn't say no to a glass of grenadine.'

'Why "this time"?' asked Marceline, rolling the last words of her question between inverted commas.

'Don't you recognize me?'

Marceline hesitated, and then owned that she did (gesture).

'Are you wondering what I've come here for at such an hour?'

'What a subtle psychologist you are, meussieu Pedro.'

'Meussieu Pedro? Why d'you call me that: "meussieu Pedro"?' the chap asked, highly intrigued, embellishing meussieu Pedro with some few inverted commas.

'Because that's what you were called this morning,' Marceline replied gently.

'Oh, was I?' said the chap airily. 'I'd forgotten.'

(silence)

'Well?' he went on, 'aren't you going to ask me what I'm doing here at this time of day?'

'No, I'm not going to ask you.'

'That's a pity,' said the chap 'because I'd have replied that I came to accept the offer of a glass of grenadine.'

Marceline started a silent little chat with herself and communicated to herself the following thought:

'He's dying for me to say that that's an idiotic excuse, but I shan't give him that pleasure, not likely.'

The chap has a look around.

'That's (gesture) where it's kept, isn't it?'

He's pointing to the sideboard, which is in the Hideous style.

As Marceline doesn't answer, he shrugs his shoulders, gets up, opens that piece of furniture, gets out the bottle and two glasses.

'You'll have a little, won't you?' he suggests.

'It'd stop me sleeping,' Marceline answers gently.

The chap doesn't insist. He drinks.

'It really is foul,' he remarks incidentally.

Marceline, for her part, makes no comment.

'So they're not back yet?' asks the chap, just to say something.

'You can see they're not. Otherwise you'd already be out on your ear.'

'Gabriella,' says the chap, dreamily (a pause). 'Killing (a pause). Positively killing.'

He finishes his glass.

'Pooh,' he mutters.

Again there is silence in the air.

Finally the chap makes up his mind.

'Ts like this,' says he, 'I've got quite a few questions to ask you.'

'Ask away,' says Marceline gently, 'but I shan't answer.'

'You'll have to,' says the chap. 'I'm Inspector Bertin Poirée.'

This makes Marceline laugh.

'Here's my card,' says the chap, annoyed.

And, from a distance, he shows it to Marceline.

'It's bogus,' says Marceline, 'you could see that with half an eye. And anyway, if you were a real inspector you'd know that's not the way to conduct an investigation. You haven't even taken the trouble to read any detective stories, French ones of course, or you'd have found that out. You've already done enough to get yourself dismissed: lock-picking, violation of the privacy of a person's domicile . . .'

'And maybe violation of something else.'

'I beg your pardon?' asked Marceline gently.

'Well it's like this,' said the chap. 'I've taken a hell of a fancy to you. The very moment I saw you, I said to myself: I won't be able to go on living on this earth if I don't stuff her sooner or later, so then I said to myself: might just as well be as soon as possible. I can't wait. I'm the impatient type: that's my nature. So the next thing I said to myself was: tonight'll be my chance because she, the divine beloved – that's you – will be all on her ownsome in her little nest, seeing that all the rest of the household including that half-wit, Turandot, will have gone to the Mount of Venus to admire Gabriella's antics. Gabriella! (silence). Killing (silence). Positively killing.'

'How d'you know all that?'

'Because I'm Inspector Bertin Poirée.'

'Bloody funny,' said Marceline, suddenly changing her vocabulary. 'You might as well confess that you're a bogus cop.'

'You think a cop — as you put it — isn't capable of falling in love?'

'And then you're too damn stupid.'

'There *are* some cops who aren't awfully bright.'

'Yes, but you're the tops.'

'Ida know, is that all the effect my declaration makes on you, my declaration of love?'

'You don't really expect me to take it lying down, do you, just for the asking.'

'I sincerely think that my personal charm will in the end leave you not indifferent.'

'Tell me another.'

'You'll see. Just a little conversation and my seductive powers will start to operate.'

'And what if they don't operate?'

'Then I'll just pounce on you. Nothing to it.'

'All right, have a bash. Try.'

'Oh, I've got plenty of time. It's only as a last resort that I'll use that method which it must be said my conscience doesn't entirely approve.'

'You'd better hurry up. Gabriel'll be back soon.'

'Oh no. Tonight it'll be a six in the morning do.'

'Poor Zazie,' said Marceline gently, 'she'll be terribly tired, and she's got to get the six-sixty train.'

'Zazie can go to hell. These kidettes make me sick, they're vinegary, pooh. While a beautiful person like you . . . Jeez.'

'Didn't stop you chasing her this morning, the poor little girl.'

'Snot true. I was the one that brought her back for you. And anyway my day was only just starting. But when I saw you . . .'

The nighthawk gazed at Marceline, assuming a green and yellow melancholy look, then he energetically seized the grenadine bottle and filled with this beverage a glass whose contents he then swallowed, putting the non-comestible part back on the table, as one does with the bone of the chop or the backbone of the sole.

'Poo-oo-ah,' he went, as he swallowed the drink he had himself elected and which he had just caused to suffer the expeditious treatment to which vodka is accustomed.

He wiped his sticky lips with the back of his (left) hand and, thereupon, started on his previously announced charm session.

'The thing about me,' he says casually, 'is that I'm fickle. That country chick, I wasn't interested in her in spite of her murderous stories. I'm talking about this morning now. But later on in the day, blow me if I don't bring down an old duck, a classy one, at first vision. The Baroness Mouaque. A widow. She's got me under her epidermis. In five minutes her whole life was turned upside down. I must say that at that moment I was attired in the splendid dress of a traffic policeman. I adore it. You can't possibly imagine how much I enjoy that uniform. My greatest joy is to whistle at a taxi and then get into it. The clotface at the wheel can't get over it. And I make him take me home. He's absolutely speechless, the clotface (silence). Maybe you think I'm a bit of a snob?'

'No accounting for tastes.'

'You're still not under my spell?'

'No.'

Bertin Poirée gave two or three little coughs and then continued in these terms:

'I must tell you about how I met her, the widow.'

'Don't give a damn,' said Marceline gently.

'Well anyway, I've parked her at the Mount of Venus. Personally, Gabriella's evolutions (Gabriella!), you can imagine how they unman me. But you . . . you elevate me.'

'Oh! meussieu Pedro-surplus, aren't you ashamed?'

'Ashamed . . . ashamed . . . doesn't mean a thing. Don't really have to be so refined when we're just chatting, do we? (a pause). Anyway, don't call me Pedro-surplus. It gets on my nerves. It's a monniker I invented on the spur of the moment, just like that, for Gabriella's benefit (Gabriella!), but I'm not used to it, I've never used it. Whereas I have others which suit me perfectly.'

'Such as Bertin Poirée?'

'For one. Or then again, there's the one I adopt when I clad myself in the raiment of a police constable (silence).'

He seems troubled.

'I clad myself,' he repeated mournfully. 'Is that right: I clad myself? I bade myself, yes, but: I clad myself? What do *you* think, my beautiful?'

'Well, bid yourself to beat it.'

'That is the last thing I intend to do. Well then, when I clad myself . . .'

'Disguise . . .'

'It isn't! not at all!! it isn't a disguise!!! what makes you think I'm not a real cop?'

Marceline shrugged her shoulders.

'All right, when you clad yourself, then . . .'

He looked worried. 'Clad myself, clad myself, it still doesn't sound right.'

'Look it up in the dictionary then.'

'A dictionary? but I haven't got a dictionary on me. Nor at home, either. If you think I have time to read. With all my pursuits.'

'There's one over there (gesture).'

'Hell,' said he, impressed. 'So you're an intellectual as well.'

But he didn't budge.

'I'll cladly fetch it for you,' said Marceline gently.

'Tsall right, I'll get it.'

With a suspicious look he went over to the shelf, trying not to let Marceline out of his sight. Then he engaged himself in painful study and became completely absorbed in this work.

'Ts see, *City Witt, The*. . . *Civil War, The*. . . *Clack, Miss*. . . *Clan na Gael*, an Irish secret society, see history by the well-known French scholar, Michel Presle . . . tisn't here.'

'It's not that dictionary, it's the big one.'

'Well, what's in the big one, dirty words I bet, ts have a look . . . *Clack*, chatter, gossip, a loud talk or chat; *Clack-loft*, a pulpit; *Clap*, *v.* to infect with gonorrhoea, what did I tell you, but it's not here either.'

'I told you, the big one.'

'Well, three dictionaries . . . Ah, at last some words everybody knows, *Clabber*. . . *Clachan*. . . *Clack v.*2, to remove the dirty clots from . . . Ah! got it, here it is, *Clad, v. arch.* 1579. (app. f. prec.) TO CLOTHE. Also *transf.* and *fig.* Well, what d'you know . . . to clothe . . . funny . . . very very funny . . . Just a minute though, what about to *Unclad.* . . ts have a look . . . *Unclasp.* . . *Uncle.* . . wonder what they put for Uncle Gabriella, no, they've only got Uncle Sam . . . *Unclad,* here we are, *Unclad,* arch. pa.t. and pa.pple. of UNCLOTHE. . . *Godiva unclad herself in haste.* So you say *unclad yourself,* eh. Well then,' he suddenly yelled, 'well then, my beautiful, unclad yourself. And in haste! Your birthday suit! Your birthday suit!'

And his eyes were all bloodshot. And all the more so as Marceline had no less totally than abruptly scarpered.

Using the toothing stones to help her in her descent, a suitcase in her hand, she flew down the wall with the greatest of ease, and then only had a little matter of some ten feet to jump to terminate her itinerary.

And when she got to the corner of the street she disappeared.

16

Trouscaillon had put his copper's uniform on again. In the little square not far from the Mount of Venus he was waiting, melancholious, for that establishment to close. He was pensively (so it seemed) watching a group of tramps who were sleeping on the grating of a metro shaft, relishing the mediterranean tepidity which that aperture dispenses and which a strike had not sufficed to cool. He meditated thus for a few moments on the fragility of human affairs and on the schemes of mice which gang no less aft a-gley than those of anthropoids, then he began to envy – only for a few moments, though, we mustn't egzaggerate – the fate of those outcasts, outcasts maybe but released from the weight of social obligations and mundane conventions. Trouscaillon sighed.

A louder sob echoed him, and this disturbed the Trouscaillic reverie. Wo twat twat can that be, said the Trouscaillic reverie to itself, it too putting on its copper's uniform again and, sweeping the shadows with a penetrating eye, it discovered the origin of the sonorous intervention in the person of an indivigil sitting on a bench and minding his own business. Trouscaillon approached him not without having taken the usual precautions. The tramps for their part went on sleeping, cops being all in a night's sleep to them.

The person was pretending to doze, which didn't reassure Trouscaillon but which didn't stop him on the other hand addressing him in these terms:

'What are you doing in this locality? And at so tardy an hour?'

'That any of your business?' replied the man, name of X.

Trouscaillon had in any case been asking himself the same question while he'd been reeling off his own. Yes, in what way was it his business? It was his profession that required it, the profession of his accoutrement, but since he had lost Marceline it seemed he'd had a tendency to soften the leather of his behaviour with the sperm of his desiderata. Combatting this fatal inclination, he pursued the conversation thus:

'Yes,' says he, 'it *is* my business.'

'Well,' said the man, 'in that case it's different.'

'Do you therefore authorize me to formulate once again the interrogative proposition which a few moments ago I prenounce in your presence?'

'I pronounced,' said the Unknown.

'I pronounce,' said Trouscaillon.

'I pronounced with a dee.'

'I pronounced,' said Trouscaillon at last. 'Ah! linguistics isn't my strong point. It's certainly played me some dirty tricks. Let's skip it. Well?'

'Well what?'

'My question.'

'Huh,' said the other, 'I've forgotten what it was. After all this time.'

'Have I got to start all over again, then?'

'Imagine so.'

'What a bore.'

Trouscaillon refrained from sighing, fearing a reaction on the part of his interlocutor.

'Come on,' said the latter cordially, 'make just a little effort.'

Trouscaillon made a hell of a big one.

'Surname christian names date of birth place of birth social security registration number number of bank account post-office savings book rent receipt water-rate receipt gas receipt electricity receipt metro season ticket bus season ticket hire-purchase bill refrigerator brochure key ring ration books paper signed in blank permit papal bull and tutti frutti hand over your papers and cut the cackle. And what's more I'm ignoring the question of motor vehicles registration book safety lantern international passport and tutti quanti because all that lot must be beyond your means.'

'Do you see the coach (gesture) over there, Officer?'

'Yes.'

'I'm its driver.'

'Ah.'

'Well, look here, you're not very bright. Haven't you recognised me yet?'

Trouscaillon, slightly reassured, went and sat down by his side.

'May I?' he asked.

'By all means.'

'The thing is, it's against the regulations.'

(silence)

'I must say, though,' went on Trouscaillon, 'far as regulations are concerned, I certainly put my foot right in it today.'

'Trifles?'

'Suet puddings.'

(silence)

Trouscaillon added:

'Cherchez la femme.'

(silence)

Trouscaillon went on:

'. . . I've got a confession that's choking my gullet . . . a confession . . . well, an epicacuanha, eh . . . at any rate, I really have got quite a bit to natter about . . .'

(silence)

'Of course,' said Fyodor Balanovitch.

A mosquito flew into the luminescent conicality of a street lamp. It wanted to warm itself up before it stung some more skins. It succeeded. Its calcinated corpse slowly descended on to the yellow asphalt.

'Well, get on with it,' said Fyodor Balanovitch, 'otherwise I shall do the talking.'

'No, no,' said Trouscaillon, 'let's go on talking about me just a bit longer.'

He scratched his scalp with a rapacious and harvesting finger-nail and then uttered some words to which he did not fail to give a certain touch of impartiality and even of nobility. Those words are these:

'I shall say nothing of my childhood or of my youth. Let us neither speak of my education, I have none, and I shall speak but little of my schooling, for I had little. On this last point, therefore, that's that. So I now arrive at my military service, on which I shall not dwell. Celibate from my earliest days, Life has made me what I am.'

He interrupted himself to indulge in a spot of day-dreaming.

'Ah well, get on with it,' said Fyodor Balanovitch. 'Otherwise I shall start.'

'No doubt about it,' said Trouscaillon, 'it's my unlucky day. And all because of the woman I encunter this morning.'

'I encountered.'

'I encounter.'

'I encountered with a dee.'

'I encountered.'

'The old trout that's tagging along after Gabriel?'

'Oh no. Not that one. Anyway, that one disappointed me. She let me go about my business, and what business, without even going through the motions of trying to stop me, all she wanted was to see Gabriella dance. Gabriella . . . bloody funny . . . really bloody funny.'

'You've said it,' said Fyodor Balanovitch. 'There's nothing like Gabriel's act in all Paris, and I can assure you I know a bit about the *bâille naïte* of this city.'

'You're lucky,' said Trouscaillon absent-mindedly.

'But I've seen it so often, Gabriel's act, that I'm fed up with it by now, and how I am. And then, he doesn't seem to get any new ideas. Artists, it can't be helped, it often happens like that. When they've found a gimmick they make the most of it. Have to admit that we're all a bit like that, everyone in his own way.'

'Not me,' said Trouscaillon with simplicity. 'My gimmicks, I'm always changing them.'

'Because you haven't found the right one yet. The thing is, you're trying to find yourself. But once you achieve some appreciable result, you'll stick to it. Because so far any results you may have achieved can't have been very extraordinary. Only just have to look at you: you're pathetic.'

'Even in my uniform?'

'It doesn't help.'

Overwhelmed, Trouscaillon fell silent.

'And,' went on Fyodor Balanovitch, 'what's the point of it?'

'I don't know really. I'm waiting for Madame Mouaque.'

'Well *I*'m quite simply waiting for my clots to take them back to their inn for they have to leave at crack of dawn tomorrow for Gibraltar, city of ancient parapets. Such is their itinerary.'

'They're lucky,' muttered Trouscaillon absent-mindedly.

Fyodor Balanovitch shrugged his shoulders and didn't deign to comment on this remark.

It was then that a hubbub made itself heard: the Mount of Venus was closing.

'Not before it was time,' said Fyodor Balanovitch.

He gets up and goes over towards his coach. He leaves like that, without any polite leave-taking.

Then Trouscaillon too gets up. He hesitates. The tramps are asleep. The mosquito is dead.

Fyodor Balanovitch gives a few toots on his horn to collect his lambs. The latter are congratulating themselves on the lovely, the excellent evening they've had and out-gibberishing each other in the effort to transmit this message in the autochthonous language. Goodbyes are said. The feminine element wants to kiss Gabriel, the masculine doesn't dare.

'A bit less hullabaloo,' says the admiral.

The travellers climb into the coach little by little. Fyodor Balanovitch yawns.

In his cage, at the end of Turandot's arm, Laverdure has fallen asleep. Zazie is resisting bravely: she's not going to copy Laverdure. Charles has gone to fetch his machine.

'Well, my fine fellow,' says the widow Mouaque, seeing Trouscaillon come up, 'have you been enjoying yourself?'

'Not overmuch, not overmuch,' says Trouscaillon.

'We've had a simply *wonderful* time. Meussieu is so *amusing*.'

'Thank you,' says Gabriel. 'Don't forget the art in it though. It's not only fun and games, it's art as well.'

'He's taking his time, fetching his jalopy,' says Turandot.

'Did she enjoy herself?' asks the admiral looking at the animal who has his beak under his wing.

'He'll have something to remember,' says Turandot.

The last travellers have found their seats. They'll send picture postcards (gestures).

'Ho ho!' cries Gabriel, 'adios amigos, chin chin, be seeing you . . .'

And the coach moves off, bearing with it the delighted foreigners. This very same day, at the crack of dawn, they'll leave for Gibraltar, city of ancient parapets. Such is their itinerary.

Charles' taxi draws up at the kerb.

'There's too many of us,' remarks Zazie.

'That doesn't matter in the least,' says Gabriel, 'now we'll go and treat ourselves to some onion soup.'

'No thanks,' says Charles. 'I'm going home.'

No two ways about it.

'Well, Mado, you coming?'

Madeleine gets in and sits beside her intended.

'Goodbye all,' she calls out of the window, 'and thank you for the lovely . . . and thank you for the ec . . .'

But nobody hears the rest. The taxi's already quite a way off.

'If we were in America,' said Gabriel, 'we'd have chucked rice at them.'

'You must have seen that in old films,' said Zazie. 'Nowadays they don't live happily ever after so much as they did in your day. Personally I prefer it when they all die.'

'I like the rice better,' said the widow Mouaque.

'Nobody rang for you,' said Zazie.

'Mademoiselle,' said Trouscaillon 'you ought to be more polite to an old lady.'

'Isn't he lovely when he stands up for me,' said the widow Mouaque.

'Let's get going,' said Gabriel. 'I'm taking you to the Queen of the Night. That's the place I'm best known at.'

The widow Mouaque and Trouscaillon follow the crowd.

'See them?' said Zazie to Gabriel, 'the old bag and the cop hanging on to us by the short hairs?'

'Can't stop 'em,' said Gabriel. 'It's a free country.'

'Can't you scare them off? I just don't want to see them any more.'

'You must show more human understanding than that in this life.'

'A cop,' said the widow Mouaque, who'd heard everything, 'is, nevertheless, a man.'

'I'd like to stand a round,' said Trouscaillon shyly.

'Ah,' said Gabriel, 'nothing doing. Tonight it's on me.'

'Just a very little round,' said Trouscaillon in a beseeching voice. 'Some muscadet, for egzample. Something within my means.'

'You don't want to make a hole in your dowry,' said Gabriel, 'it's different for me.'

'Furthermore,' said Turandot, 'you're not going to stand us anything at all. You forget you're a cop. I'm in the trade, I'd never serve a cop who brought a gang of people with him to wet their whistles.'

'You aren't very bright,' said Gridoux. 'Don't you recognize him? He's this morning's sex-maniac.'

Gabriel leant over to egzamine him more carefully. Everyone, even Zazie because she was both highly surprised and annoyed, awaited the result of this inspection. Trouscaillon was the first to preserve a prudent silence.

'What've you done with your whiskers?' Gabriel asked him, in a voice which was at the same time calm and awe-inspiring.

'You're not going to hurt him,' said the widow Mouaque.

With one hand Gabriel seized Trouscaillon by the lapel and took him over to the light of a street lamp to complete his study.

'Yes,' he said. 'What about your whiskers?'

'I left them at home,' said Trouscaillon.

'So you really *are* a cop, then, into the bargain?'

'No, no,' cried Trouscaillon. 'It's a disguise . . . just to amuse myself . . . to amuse you . . . it's like your tutu . . . it's the same thing . . . it's six of one and half a dozen of the other . . .'

'Half a dozen of the best for you,' said Gridoux, inspired.

'Yes but still you're not going to hurt him,' said the widow Mouaque.

'This needs some explanation,' said Turandot, getting over his misgivings.

'Talk, talk . . .' Laverdure said feebly, and went back to sleep.

Zazie kept her trap shut. Events had got beyond her, she was overcome by somnolence, and she was trying to find an attitude which would be adequate both to the situation and to her personal dignity, but she couldn't make it.

Hoisting Trouscaillon up the street lamp, Gabriel again looked at him in silence, delicately replaced him on his feet and addressed him in these terms:

'And what're you doing following us like this?'

'It's not you he's following,' said the widow Mouaque, 'it's me.'

'That's right,' said Trouscaillon. 'Perhaps you don't know how it is, but when you've got an itch for a doll . . .'

'What're you (oh isn't he sweet) insinuating (he called me) about my private life (a doll),' said, synchronically, Gabriel (and the widow Mouaque), the one furiously, (the other fervently).

'You poor fish,' Gabriel went on, turning to the lady, 'he doesn't tell *you* all he does.'

'I haven't had time yet,' said Trouscaillon.

'He's a disgusting sex-maniac,' said Gabriel. 'This morning he followed Zazie all the way home. Unspeakable.'

'Did you do that?' asked the widow Mouaque, upset.

'I didn't know you then,' said Trouscaillon.

'He admits it!' yelled the widow Mouaque.

'He's admitted it!' yelled Turandot and Gridoux.

'Ah! you admit it!' said Gabriel in a loud voice.

'Forgive me!' cried Trouscaillon, 'forgive me!'

'The bastard!' bawled the widow Mouaque.

These vociferous exclamations caused two bicyclorized cops to loom up out of the darkness.

'Disturbance of the peace at night!' they yelled, the two bicyclorized cops, that is, 'lunar rough-housing, somniverous hullabalooing, bawling medianoche, huh, think you're going to,' they yelled, the two bicyclorized cops, that is.

Gabriel, discreetly, stopped holding Trouscaillon by his lapels.

'Sta minute,' exclaimed Trouscaillon displaying the greatest courage, 'sta minute, didn't you see me? Adspick at my uniform. I'm a
copper-man, look at my wings.'

And he flapped his cloak up and down.

'And where do *you* spring from,' said the bicyclorised cop qualified
to initiate the colloquy. 'Vnever seen you round these parts.'

'Possible,' replied Trouscaillon animated by an audacity that a
good writer could only describe as insane. 'Possible, nevertheless a
cop I am, a cop I remain.'

'But that lot,' said the bicycop slyly, 'that lot (gesture), they all
cops too?'

'Oh you wouldn't want that. But they're as sweet as hyssop.'

'This doesn't seem very orthodox to me,' said the bicycop who
could talk.

The other contented himself with making faces. Terrifying.

'I've made my first communion, though,' retorted Trouscaillon.

'Well that's a thought that doesn't smell very copperlike,' exclaimed
the bicycop who could talk. 'I scent a reader of those seditious
publications that try to make people believe in the union of the
aspergillum and the truncheon. Well now, let me tell you (and he
addresses his remarks to the whole lot of them), curés, the police
know where to put them (gesture).'

This dumb show was welcomed with reserve, except by Turandot
who smiled subserviently. Gabriel shrugged his shoulders somewhat
obviously.

'You,' the bicycop who could talk said to him, 'stink (a pause).
Of marjoram.'

'Marjoram,' cried Gabriel pityingly. 'It's Fior's Barbouze.'

'Oh!' said the bicycop incredulously. 'Tsava look-see.'

He went over and sniffed Gabriel's jacket.

'My goodness,' he then said, almost convinced. 'Come and have
a look-see,' he added to his colleague.

So then the other started sniffing Gabriel's jacket.

He nodded.

'But,' said the one who could talk, 'he needn't think I'm so easily
mugged. He stinks of marjoram.'

'I wonder what these bleeding oafs can possibly know about it,' said Zazie, yawning.

'Crikey,' said the bicycop who could talk, 'did you hear that, subordinate? That sounds like slander to me. How can we now waive the exercise of our duty?'

'Wave away,' said Zazie languidly, 'so long as you don't make it a permanent one.'

And as Gabriel and Gridoux were guffawing, she added for their information and amusement:

'I found that one in the Memoirs of General Vermot, too.'

'Ah well so now,' said the bicycop. 'Here's a young chick taking the mickey out of us like that chap with his marjoram.'

'It is not,' said Gabriel. 'I tell you it's Fior's Barbouze.'

Now it was the widow Mouaque's turn to go up and sniff him.

'It is too,' she said to the two bicycops.

'Nobody rang for you,' said the one who couldn't talk.

'That's true enough,' mumbled Zazie. 'I told her that already, earlier on.'

'Really should have a little try to be polite to the lady,' said Trouscaillon.

'You,' said the bicycop who could talk, 'would do better not to draw too much attention to your own sweet self.'

'Really should have a little try,' repeated Trouscaillon with a courage which touched the widow Mouaque.

'Wouldn't you be better off in bed at this our?'

'Ha ha,' said Zazie.

'Let's have a look at your papers then,' the bicycop who could talk said to Trouscaillon.

'Never heard of such a thing,' said the widow Mouaque.

'You over there, the old woman, shut your trap,' said the bicycop who couldn't talk.

'Be polite to the lady,' said Trouscaillon who was becoming foolhardy.

'Another non-coplike remark,' said the bicycop who could talk. 'Your papers,' he yelled, 'and get a jerk on.'

'Oh what a laugh,' said Zazie.

'Just the same it's a bit much,' said Trouscaillon. 'You ask *me* for my papers now and you don't ask these people (gesture) for anything.'

'Now that,' said Gabriel, 'is not nice.'

'What a louse,' said Gridoux.

But the bicycops weren't going to be put off as easily as all that.

'Your papers,' yelled the one who could talk.

'Your papers,' yelled the one who couldn't.

'Disturbance of the peace at night,' superyelled at this moment some new cops, this lot complete with a Black Maria. 'Lunar rough-housing, somniverous hullabalooing, bawling medianoche, huh, think you're going to . . .'

With perfect flair they smelt out those responsible and without a moment's hesitation embarked Trouscaillon and the two bicycops. The whole lot disappeared in a second.

'There is *some* justice after all,' said Gabriel.

As for the widow Mouaque, she was lamenting.

'Mustn't cry,' said Gabriel. 'There was something bordering on the phoney about your boyo. And anyway we'd had enough of his shadowing us. Cheer up, come and have some onion soup with us. The onion soup that soothes and consoles.'

17

A tear fell on to a scalding-hot croûton and there evaporated.

'Come on, cheer up,' said Gabriel to the widow Mouaque, 'pull yourself together. There's as many fish in the sea as ever came out of it. Fright though you are, you won't have any trouble in hooking another boy-friend.'

She sighs dubiously. The croûton slips into the spoon and the widow projects it, steaming, into her oesophagus. She suffers therefrom.

'Call the fire brigade,' says Gabriel.

And he refills her glass for her. Each mouaquian mouthful is thus washed down by the harsh muscadet.

Zazie has joined Laverdure in somnia. Gridoux and Turandot are silently struggling with the strings of melted cheese.

'Terrific, eh,' Gabriel says to them, 'this onion soup. Anyone'd think that you (gesture) had put in some soles and heels and you (gesture) had saved up your washing-up water for them. But that's what I like: sweet simplicity, the light of nature. Purity, eh.'

The others nod, but without comment.

'Well Zazie, aren't you going to eat your soup?'

'Let her sleep,' said the widow Mouaque in a prostrate voice. 'Let her dream.'

Zazie opens one eye.

'Huh,' says she, 'is the old hag still there.'

'You should pity the unfortunate,' said Gabriel.

'You're very kind,' said the widow Mouaque. 'Not like her (gesture). Children, it's a well-known fact: they're heartless.'

She emptied her glass and indicated to Gabriel that she eagerly desired him to refill it.

'Lot of tripe she talks,' said Zazie feebly.

'Pah,' said Gabriel. 'What's it matter? Eh, old crock?' he added, addressing himself to the most directly interested party.

'Ah, you're kind,' said the latter. 'Not like her. Children, it's a well-known fact. They're heartless.'

'How much longer's she going to nauseate us?' Turandot asked Gabriel, taking advantage of a successful act of deglutition.

'Well you are hard-hearted,' said Gabriel. 'After all she's upset, the old wreck.'

'Thank you,' said the widow Mouaque effusively.

'Don't mention it,' said Gabriel. 'And to come back to this onion soup, it must be admitted that it's a most remarkable invention.'

'This one,' asked Gridoux who, having consummated his consumption was energetically scraping the bottom of his plate to break down the resistance of the gruyère that was still sticking to the crockery, 'this soup in particular or onion soup in general?'

'In general,' replied Gabriel decisively. 'I always talk in general. No half-measures for me.'

'You're right,' said Turandot who had also finished his skilly, 'mustn't overlook the obvious. Egzample: the muscadet is making itself scarce, the old girl's swigging the lot.'

'That's because it's really not bad,' said the widow Mouaque, smiling blissfully. '*I* can talk in general too, when I want to.'

'Talk, talk,' said Laverdure waking up with a start for a reason unknown to all and to himself, 'that's all you can do.'

'I've had enough,' said Zazie, pushing away her portion.

'Wait a minute,' said Gabriel, eagerly grabbing her plate, 'I'll finish it for you. And bring us two bottles of muscadet and one of grenadine,' he added to a waiter who was cruising in the vicinity. 'And him (gesture), we're forgetting him. Maybe he'd like a bite of something?'

'Hey, Laverdure,' said Turandot, 'you hungry?'

'Talk, talk,' said Laverdure, 'that's all you can do.'

'That,' said Gridoux, 'means yes.'

'I don't need you to teach me to understand what he says,' said Turandot haughtily.

'I wouldn't take that liberty,' said Gridoux.

'Yes but he did,' said the widow Mouaque.

'Don't make matters worse,' said Gabriel.

'You understand,' Turandot said to Gridoux, 'I understand what you understand just as well as you do. I'm no more of a stupid bastard than the next fellow.'

'If you understand as much as I do,' said Gridoux, 'then you're less of a stupid bastard than you look.'

'And talking about looking like one,' said the widow Mouaque, 'he certainly looks like one.'

'She's got a nerve,' said Turandot. 'Starting to anathemize me now.'

'You see what happens when you haven't any prestige,' said Gridoux. 'The most insignificant clot-hound spits right in your face. She wouldn't dare do it to me.'

'Everybody is a stupid bastard,' said the widow Mouaque with sudden energy. 'Including you,' she added, to Gridoux.

She immediately received a smart clip.

She returned it no less nimbly.

But Gridoux had another one in reserve, which rang out on the Mouaquian face.

"Od's blood!' yelled Turandot.

And he started skipping about in between the tables, vaguely trying to imitate Gabriella in *The Dying Swan*.

Zazie was asleep again. Laverdure, in a spirit of vengeance, no doubt, was trying to eject from his cage a piece of fresh excrement.

Meanwhile slaps were travelling thick and fast between Gridoux and the widow Mouaque, and Gabriel was guffawing at the sight of Turandot trying to shake a leg.

But all this was not to the taste of the waiters of the Queen of Night. Two of them, specialists in goings-on of this sort, suddenly seized Turandot, each under one arm, and, blithely holding him between them, it didn't take them a minute to project him on to the asphalted carriage-way, thus interrupting the cruising of several morose taxis in the greyish and fresh air of the early dawn.

'Well that,' said Gabriel. 'Well, no; can't have that.'

He got up and, grabbing hold of the two waiters who were

returning, satisfied, to their domestic pursuits, he cracked their nuts together with such force and in such fine fashion that the two fops lapsed into collapse.

'Bravo!' chorused Gridoux and the widow Mouaque who, with common accord, had interrupted their exchange of correspondence.

A third waiter, who knew his way around when it came to brawls, thought he'd achieve a lightning victory. Picking up a syphon he purposed to cause its mass to reverberate against Gabriel's skull. But Gridoux had foreseen the counter-offensive. Another syphon, no less compact, which he was instrumental in chucking, succeeded, at the conclusion of its trajectory, in wreaking havoc on the clever-guts's little head.

"Od's blood!' yells Turandot who, having recovered his equilibrium on the carriage-way at the expense of the brakes of a few particularly matutinal nocturnal carriages, was once more making his way into the brasserie and showing a fine desire for combat.

And now whole flocks of waiters loomed up from all directions. You'd neverv believed there couldv been so many. They came out of kitchens, cellars, pantries, store-rooms. Their serried ranks absorbed Gridoux and then Turandot who'd ventured among them. But they couldn't manage to reduce Gabriel so easily. Like unto the coleopter attacked by a myrmidonian column, like unto the ox assailed by a hirudinal shoal, Gabriel shook himself, squirmed and squiggled, projecting in different directions various human projectiles which flew through the air and ended up by breaking tables and chairs or rolling in between the feet of the customers.

The noise of this controversy finally woke Zazie. Perceiving her uncle a prey to the victualling mob, she bawled out: Come on, unkoo! and grabbing hold of a carafe full of water, threw it at random into the fray. So strong is the martial spirit among the daughters of France. Following this example, the widow Mouaque disseminated ash trays all about her. So powerful is the spirit of imitation that it can cause even the least gifted to act. Then was heard a considerable fracas: Gabriel had just collapsed into the crockery, carrying with him into the debris seven waiters who were completely out of control, five customers who had been taking part and one epileptic.

Rising to their feet with a simultaneous impulse, Zazie and the widow Mouaque approached the human magma which was struggling in the sawdust and crockery. A few judiciously applied blows with a syphon eliminated from the competition several persons endowed with fragile skulls. Thanks to which Gabriel was able to pick himself up, thus tearing asunder, as you might say, the curtain formed by his adversaries, and at the same time revealing the damaged presence of Gridoux and Turandot prostrate on the ground. A few aquagaseous jets directed on to their noddles by the feminine and ministering angel element put them back into circulation. From then on, the issue of the combat was no longer in doubt.

While the tepid or indifferent customers were discreetly making themselves scarce, the assiduous ones and the waiters, puffing and blowing, were wilting under Gabriel's severe fist, Gridoux's stupefying judo throws and Turandot's virulent foot. When they were reduced to a frazzle, Zazie and Mouaque effaced them from the surface of the Queen of the Night and dragged them on to the pavement where benevolent amateurs, out of pure kindness of heart, piled them all up in a heap. The only one to take no part in the hecatomb was Laverdure who, at the very beginning of hostilities, had been painfully wounded in the perineum by a bit of a soup-tureen. Lying helpless at the bottom of his cage he was murmuring as he groaned: 'charming evening, charming evening'; traumatized, he'd changed his tune.

Even without his assistance, victory was soon total.

When the last antagonist had been eliminated, Gabriel rubbed his hands with satisfaction and said:

'I could do with a coffee, now.'

'Good idea,' said Turandot, and he went behind the counter while the others leant against it.

'What about Laverdure?'

Turandot set off in search of the animal whom he found still cursing. He took him out of his cage and started to caress him, calling him his little green chicken. Laverdure, restored to equanimity, replied:

'Talk talk, that's all you can do.'

'That's true enough,' said Gabriel. 'What about that coffee?'

Reassured, Turandot re-encaged the parrot and went over to the machine. He tried to make it work, but, not being used to that model, he began by scalding his hand.

'Owowowch,' said he, in all simplicity.

'Clumsy idiot,' said Gridoux.

'Poor darling,' said the widow Mouaque.

'Blast,' said Turandot.

'The coffee,' said Gabriel: 'very white for me.'

'And I'll have mine,' said Zazie, 'with a skin on.'

'Aaaaaaahh,' replied Turandot who'd just sent a jet of steam right into his own mug.

'We'd do better to ask someone who belongs to the establishment,' said Gabriel placidly.

'Good idea,' said Gridoux, 'I'll go and fetch one.'

He went and chose from the pile the least damaged one. Whom he towed in.

'You were fabulous, you know,' Zazie said to Gabriel. 'Hormosessuals like you, I don't reckon they come by the dozen.'

'And how would mademoiselle like her coffee?' asked the waiter who'd been brought to his senses.

'With a skin on,' said Zazie.

'Why do you insist on calling me a hormosessual?' asked Gabriel calmly. 'Now that you've seen me at the Mount of Venus, you ought to know better.'

'Hormosessual or not,' said Zazie 'at any rate you were really supreme.'

'Well you see,' said Gabriel, 'I didn't like their behaviour (gesture).'

'Oh meussieu,' said the waiter thus indicated, 'we're awfully sorry, really we are.'

'The thing is they'd insulted me,' said Gabriel.

'There, meussieu,' said the waiter, 'you are mistaken.'

'They had though,' said Gabriel.

'Don't let it worry you,' said Gridoux, 'one's always being insulted by someone.'

'That's a thought,' said Turandot.

'And now,' Gridoux asked Gabriel, 'what were you thinking of doing?'

'Well, drinking this coffee.'

'And then?'

'Dropping in at home and then taking Zazie to the station.'

'Have you seen outside?'

'No.'

'Well then, go and have a look.'

Gabriel went.

'Yerss,' he said, coming back.

Two armoured divisions of night-watchmen and a squadron of jurassic spahis had just in fact taken up their position all round the place Pigalle.

18

'Maybe I ought to ring Marceline,' said Gabriel.

The others went on drinking their coffee in silence.

'Now the squit's going to fly,' said the waiter under his breath.

'Nobody rang for you,' retorted the widow Mouaque.

'I'll take you back where I got you from,' said Gridoux.

'All right all right,' said the waiter, 'can't even make a joke any more.'

Gabriel came back.

'It's funny,' says he. 'Zno answer.'

He started to drink his coffee.

'Hell,' he added, 'it's cold.'

He put it down on the counter, disgusted.

Gridoux went to have a look.

'They're coming nearer,' he announced.

Abandoning the counter, the others clustered round him, except for the waiter who camouflaged himself beneath the cash desk.

'They don't look all that pleased,' remarked Gabriel.

'This is fabulous,' murmured Zazie.

'I hope nothing happens to Laverdure,' said Turandot. '*He* hasn't done anything.'

'What about me then,' said the widow Mouaque. 'What've *I* done?'

'You can go and join your Trouscaillon,' said Gridoux, shrugging his shoulders.

'There he is, though!' she exclaimed.

Stepping over the pile of the crestfallen who constituted a sort of barricade in front of the entrance to the Queen of the Night, the widow Mouaque showed signs of intending to throw herself on the assailants who were advancing with deliberation and precision. A good fistful of tommy-gun bullets cut short this tentative. The widow Mouaque, holding her guts in her hands, collapsed.

'How silly,' she murmured. 'And me with a private income.'

And she dies.

'Things are deteriorating,' observed Turandot. 'I do hope Laverdure doesn't get hurt.'

Zazie had fainted.

'They ought to watch what they're doing,' said Gabriel, furious. 'There's children present.'

'You'll be able to make your remarks to them,' said Gridoux. 'Here they are.'

These gentlemen, heavily armed, were now quite simply just the other side of the windows, a defence that was all the weaker in that they had for the most part busted during the preceding brawl. These gentlemen, heavily armed, came to a halt, in line, in the middle of the pavement. An individual, his brolly hanging from his arm, detached himself from the group and, stepping over the corpse of the widow Mouaque, entered the brasserie.

'Good God,' chorused Gabriel, Turandot, Gridoux and Laverdure.

Zazie was still in a faint.

'Yes,' said the man with the (new) brolly, 'it is I, Haroun al Rations. I am I, he whom you cognized and, at times, hardly recognised. Prince of this world and of several related territories, I take pleasure in traversing my domain under various guises, taking on the appearances of incertitude and error which, in any case, are mine own. Primary and defalcatory policeman, noctivagant miscreant, irresolute pursuer of widows and orphans, these fleeting images allow me to assume without apprehension the minor risks of ridicule, of absurdity, and of sentimental effusion (noble gesture in the direction of the late widow Mouaque). Scarcely have I been posted missing by your indifferent consciences than I reappear as the conquering hero, and that without the slightest modesty. See! (Another gesture, no less noble but this time embracing the situation as a whole).'

'Talk, talk,' said Laverdure, 'that's . . .'

'Just about ready for the stewpan, that thing, I should say,' says Trouscaillon, sorry, Haroun al Rations.

'Never,' cried Turandot, clasping the cage to his heart. 'To perish rather! . . .'

With these words he starts to be swallowed up and lost in the wide womb of uncreated night, or the bowels of the earth, rather, and so do Gabriel, Zazie and Gridoux for that matter. The goods-lift takes the whole lot down into the Queen of the Night's cellar. The operator of the goods-lift, immersed in obscurity, told them gently, but firmly, to follow him and to make it snappy. He was waving a torch, at the same time a rallying signal and a token of the signal virtues of the battery which sustained it. While on the ground floor the heavily armed gentlemen, under the influence of emotion, were letting off bursts of tommy-gun fire into each other's legs, the little group, following the above-mentioned injunction and light, were progressing with appreciable rapidity among the racks crammed full of bottles of muscadine and grenadet. Gabriel was carrying Zazie, still in a faint, Turandot Laverdure, still disgruntled, and Gridoux wasn't carrying anything.

They went down some stairs, then they crossed the threshold of a little door and found themselves in a sewer. A bit further on they crossed the threshold of another little door and found themselves in a corridor lined with glazed bricks, still dark and deserted.

'Now,' said the lampadephore gently, 'if we don't want to be spotted, we must separate. You,' he added addressing himself to Turandot, ''ll have some trouble with your birdie.'

'I'll paint him black,' said Turandot darkly.

'All this,' said Gabriel, 'is not very funny.'

'Good old Gabriel,' said Gridoux, 'he will have his little joke.'

'I,' said the lampadephore, ''ll take the child. You too, Gabriel, are somewhat visible. Anyway I brought her suitcase with me. But I've probably left some of her things behind. I was in a hurry.'

'Tell me what happened.'

'This isn't the moment.'

The lights came on.

'There you are,' said the other gently. 'The metro's working again. You, Gridoux take the Etoile line and you, Turandot, the Bastille line.'

'And we'll do the best we can?' said Turandot.

'If you haven't got any blacking on you,' said Gabriel, 'you're going to have to use your imagination.'

'What if I put myself in the cage,' said Turandot, 'and get Laverdure to carry me?'

'That's an idea.'

'I,' said Gridoux, 'shall go home. The shoe trade, fortunately, is one of the foundations of society. And what distinguishes one cobbler from another cobbler?'

'Stands to reason.'

'Goodbye then, you lot!' said Gridoux.

And he moved off towards the Etoile line.

'Goodbye then, you lot,' said Laverdure.

'Talk, talk,' said Turandot, 'that's all you can do.'

And they took wing towards the Bastille line.

Jeanne Lalochère woke up with a start. She consulted her wrist watch which was on the table by the bed; it was past six o'clock.

'I mustn't hang around.'

She lingered a few instants, nevertheless, to examine her boyo who was naked and snoring. She looked at him in general and then in particular, considering especially, with lassitude and placidity, the object which had so occupied her during one day and two nights, and which now looked more like a baby after its feed than a lusty young grenadier.

'And he's so stupid, too.'

She dressed in haste, threw various objects into her hold-all, sploshed some make-up on to her face.

'I mustn't be late. If I want to retrieve the girl. If I know Gabriel. They're bound to be on time. Unless anything's happened to her.'

She clasped her lipstick to her heart.

'I hope nothing *has* happened to her.'

Now she was quite ready. She looked at her boyo once more.

'If he comes to see me. If he insists. Perhaps I won't say no. But I'm not going to chase him any more.'

She shut the door gently behind her. The hotel man called her a taxi and at the half hour she was at the station. She left some things on two corner seats and got out on to the platform again. Not long afterwards, up came Zazie accompanied by a chap who was carrying her suitcase for her.

'Well,' said Jeanne Lalochère. 'Marcel.'

'As you see.'

'But she's asleep on her feet!'

'We had a little party. You must excuse her. And me too, you must excuse me if I beat it.'

'I understand. But what about Gabriel?'

'Could be better. I'm off. Bye, Zazie.'

'Goodbye, meussieu,' said Zazie, miles away.

Jeanne Lalochère got her into the compartment.

'Well, did you enjoy yourself?'

'All right.'

'Did you see the metro?'

'No.'

'What *have* you done, then?'

'I've aged.'

FOR THE BEST IN PAPERBACKS, LOOK FOR THE

In every corner of the world, on every subject under the sun, Penguin represents quality and variety—the very best in publishing today.

For complete information about books available from Penguin—including Puffins, Penguin Classics, and Compass—and how to order them, write to us at the appropriate address below. Please note that for copyright reasons the selection of books varies from country to country.

In the United Kingdom: Please write to *Dept. EP, Penguin Books Ltd, Bath Road, Harmondsworth, West Drayton, Middlesex UB7 0DA.*

In the United States: Please write to *Penguin Putnam Inc., P.O. Box 12289 Dept. B, Newark, New Jersey 07101-5289* or call 1-800-788-6262.

In Canada: Please write to *Penguin Books Canada Ltd, 10 Alcorn Avenue, Suite 300, Toronto, Ontario M4V 3B2.*

In Australia: Please write to *Penguin Books Australia Ltd, P.O. Box 257, Ringwood, Victoria 3134.*

In New Zealand: Please write to *Penguin Books (NZ) Ltd, Private Bag 102902, North Shore Mail Centre, Auckland 10.*

In India: Please write to *Penguin Books India Pvt Ltd, 11 Panchsheel Shopping Centre, Panchsheel Park, New Delhi 110 017.*

In the Netherlands: Please write to *Penguin Books Netherlands bv, Postbus 3507, NL-1001 AH Amsterdam.*

In Germany: Please write to *Penguin Books Deutschland GmbH, Metzlerstrasse 26, 60594 Frankfurt am Main.*

In Spain: Please write to *Penguin Books S. A., Bravo Murillo 19, 1° B, 28015 Madrid.*

In Italy: Please write to *Penguin Italia s.r.l., Via Benedetto Croce 2, 20094 Corsico, Milano.*

In France: Please write to *Penguin France, Le Carré Wilson, 62 rue Benjamin Baillaud, 31500 Toulouse.*

In Japan: Please write to *Penguin Books Japan Ltd, Kaneko Building, 2-3-25 Koraku, Bunkyo-Ku, Tokyo 112.*

In South Africa: Please write to *Penguin Books South Africa (Pty) Ltd, Private Bag X14, Parkview, 2122 Johannesburg.*